Olive and the Bitter Herbs

by Charles Busch

A SAMUEL FRENCH ACTING EDITION

SAMUEL FRENCH

FOUNDED 1830

NEW YORK HOLLYWOOD LONDON TORONTO

SAMUELFRENCH.COM

ISBN 978-0-573-70007-1   Printed in U.S.A.   #28121

MUSIC USE NOTE

Licensees are solely responsible for obtaining formal written permission from copyright owners to use copyrighted music in the performance of this play and are strongly cautioned to do so. If no such permission is obtained by the licensee, then the licensee must use only original music that the licensee owns and controls. Licensees are solely responsible and liable for all music clearances and shall indemnify the copyright owners of the play and their licensing agent, Samuel French, Inc., against any costs, expenses, losses and liabilities arising from the use of music by licensees.

IMPORTANT BILLING AND CREDIT
REQUIREMENTS

All producers of *OLIVE AND THE BITTER HERBS must* give credit to the Author of the Play in all programs distributed in connection with performances of the Play, and in all instances in which the title of the Play appears for the purposes of advertising, publicizing or otherwise exploiting the Play and/or a production. The name of the Author *must* appear on a separate line on which no other name appears, immediately following the title and *must* appear in size of type not less than fifty percent of the size of the title type.

In addition the following credit *must* be given in all programs and publicity information distributed in association with this piece:

World Premiere produced in New York City by Primary Stages in association with Daryl Roth and Bob Boyett. Opening night-August 16, 2011.

Olive and the Bitter Herbs **was commissioned by Primary Stages.**

OLIVE AND THE BITTER HERBS was first produced by Primary Stages - 59E59 Theatre (Andrew Leynse, Artistic Director) in New York City on July 26, 2011. The performance was directed by Mark Brokaw, with sets by Anna Louizos, costumes by Suzy Benzinger, lighting by Mary Louis Geiger, and sound and original music by John Gromada. The production stage manager was William H. Lang. The cast was as follows:

OLIVE . . . . Marcia Jean Kurtz

WENDY . . . . Julie Halston

TREY . . . . .Dan Butler

SYLVAN . . . . Richard Masur

ROBERT . . . . David Garrison

CHARACTERS

OLIVE
WENDY
TREY
ROBERT
SYLVAN

PROLOGUE

(Olive's apartment living room in the East Thirties in Manhattan. There is a large decorative mirror on one side of the room and another mirror hanging on an opposite wall over the desk. Two in the morning. The room is dark except for the street lights coming in through the window.)

(OLIVE, a woman in her seventies, enters from the bedroom in her night gown. She crosses the living room and exits into the kitchen. We see the spill from the kitchen light and hear her opening a cabinet. The kitchen light goes off. OLIVE leaves the kitchen holding a box of Ritz crackers. As she returns to her bedroom, her eyes meet her reflection in the large decorative mirror. Something attracts her attention. She squints not sure of what she's seeing. She moves closer to the mirror searching for something beyond her reflection.)

OLIVE. Don't go. Please, don't go. I'm not afraid.

(blackout)

7

ACT ONE

Scene One

(*Four pm.* **WENDY**, *an energetic, upbeat woman around fifty, is straightening the spread on the sofa.* **OLIVE** *enters in her housedress and slippers.* **WENDY** *and* **OLIVE** *both speak with New York accents.* **OLIVE** *is a feisty curmudgeon. To her, the glass is more than half empty; it's drained. However, she is not full of rage or mean-spirited. Despite or because of her tough, nihilistic point of view, there is something compelling about her. She has earned her living as an actress for many years but there is nothing "actressy" or theatrical about her. At heart, she's still a former bookkeeper from Yonkers.*)

OLIVE. I sent you next door to make their lives miserable, not invite them over.

WENDY. They seem like nice people. Cultivate them. What if you have an emergency in the middle of the night?

OLIVE. They're despicable human beings.

WENDY. You've never even spoken to them.

OLIVE. Wendy, you're not in this apartment twenty-four hours a day. You never hear them at their worst. These walls are wafer thin. The opera recordings. The entertaining till nine o'clock at night. The laughter. It's been like a Nazi persecution.

WENDY. We had a lovely chat just now and I found them to be utterly charming.

OLIVE. The smell from their baked cheese should only be permeating *your* walls. They must subsist on a steady diet of eggplant parmigian and potatoes gratin. *(pronounced:* "grottin"*)*

WENDY. Olive, you're not getting me riled up. You're making me salivate.

(**WENDY** *gathers a pile of newspapers.*)

OLIVE. Hey! I haven't done the puzzle yet.

WENDY. I'm putting the papers in a nice neat pile. Just a little sprucing up.

OLIVE. They won't be here long enough to appreciate your sprucing.

WENDY. I thought things would improve when the woman upstairs moved out.

OLIVE. That was an unendurable torture. The stomping around at all hours.

WENDY. And it turned out she was a tiny dwarf.

OLIVE. That little person had thighs like Mike Tyson. In this building I'm dismissed as a chronic complainer, a crank. If I owned this apartment and wasn't the sole surviving renter, believe you me, it would be a whole different ballgame. This morning I was getting the mail and I ran into the President of the co-op board, Carol Kandel. I was calmly telling her about my situation with the monsters next door, whereupon she accused me of character assassination. I told her she was a pretentious, overly botoxed, ageist pig.

WENDY. You didn't.

OLIVE. She fancies herself an interior decorator. What she's done to this lobby is a *shandeh*. A disgrace. This is an apartment house. Not a Tuscan villa. *(She winces in pain.)* Ow.

WENDY. What's wrong?

OLIVE. When I'm in a bad mood, I immediately feel it in my metatarsals.

WENDY. Olive, I made an appointment for you to see my podiatrist, Dr. Parvati Gupta-Kapoor. It's in your date book. Next Monday at one thirty. I'll go with you.

OLIVE. You and your doctors. I should just rent a permanent suite at Beth Israel. Oh, before you leave, fix the cable box again. Off with your head if I miss my NCIS.

(**WENDY** *instinctively rolls her eyes.*)

OLIVE. I saw that. You rolled your eyes. You're very testy today.

WENDY. Just tired. I was all morning with Doris Blau. Poor thing broke her shoulder. Oh, she's a wonderful actress.

OLIVE. She can't act.

WENDY. She won a Tony Award.

OLIVE. She stinks.

WENDY. You should give her a call. She'd appreciate it.

OLIVE. We no longer speak.

WENDY. You're not speaking to half the membership of Actor's Equity. I've never known anyone with more feuds.

OLIVE. There's something in my body chemistry that provokes people to hurt me. The one time I attended the Cleo Awards, a total stranger came up to me on the red carpet and stole my wiglet. I've never picked a fight with anyone in my entire life.

WENDY. You've never picked a fight?

(**WENDY** *steps into the tiny kitchen barely offstage. They continue their conversation.*)

OLIVE. Not in my entire life. Now how many times do you want me to repeat that?

(**WENDY** *reappears with a bottle of Windex and a piece of paper towel.*)

WENDY. There's not a single person on the face of the earth who hasn't started a fight at some point.

OLIVE. I haven't but you're trying to start one right now.

WENDY. I'm just completely flummoxed by that outrageous statement.

(**WENDY** *starts to spray Windex on one of the mirrors.*)

OLIVE. Well, remain flummoxed. What the hell are you doing to that mirror?

WENDY. Giving it a breast reduction. What do you think I'm doing?

OLIVE. Put that thing down.

WENDY. Didn't Carmen dust this when she was here yesterday? This mirror is my favorite thing in the apartment. I feel as if it's somehow beckoning me. Come closer, Wendy, come closer. The frame is like a proscenium arch and within it I am, for once, the star of my own life.

OLIVE. *(alarmed)* Get away from that mirror! If I want it dusted, I'll dust it myself!

WENDY. All right. All right. You see your attitude? You're combative.

*(**WENDY** returns to the kitchen to put away the Windex.)*

OLIVE. You're confusing anger with vocal color; a sign of good theatrical training.

*(**WENDY** comes back.)*

WENDY. You know, Olive, I've always assumed you never had any formal acting lessons.

OLIVE. Well, you assumed wrong.

WENDY. Hey, maybe you should teach a course in commercial acting. You were in one of the classic commercials of all time.

OLIVE. That's the most idiotic notion you've come up with yet.

WENDY. I worry about you, Olive. I shouldn't. You're not my relative. You're not my responsibility. But I can't help getting involved. It's important to share your life with others. I feel a genuine sense of failure that I've never known the joy of marriage. I turned down several proposals. They didn't feel right.

OLIVE. We're all alone, kid. Don't fight it.

WENDY. I fight it by keeping busy. *(She points to a small notebook on the desk.)* I filled up that notebook with wonderful suggestions. I bet you've never even opened it. Number four; a Yoga class. A good one. Number five was certainly worthy of consideration. People tell me you used to be very involved in local Democratic politics.

OLIVE. Never again. The only change I believe in now are four quarters to a dollar.

WENDY. Olive, human beings *are* capable of change. It's essential. When people are static they deteriorate. Now, you've had a series of minor strokes –.

OLIVE. Hold on a minute, sister. I had two and they weren't strokes. They were episodes.

WENDY. Okay. Episodes. And thank God, you're doing marvelously. But taking a Coumadin blood thinner isn't enough. You need to pull yourself out of the mire. Embrace life.

OLIVE. ENOUGH ALL READY! I'm not helping anyone's cockamamie campaign for city council, I'm not gonna teach and I'm not sticking my ass in the air taking yoga for seniors.

(The door bell rings.)

OLIVE. SHUT UP!

WENDY. What do you want me to do?

OLIVE. Let them in if you want. I could care less.

*(***WENDY*** *opens the door.)*

WENDY. Hello! It's been a lifetime! Fifteen minutes! Come in.

*(***ROBERT*** *and* ***TREY*** *enter.* ***ROBERT*** *is an attractive man around sixty and* ***TREY***, *a sour pickle, drinking from a beer bottle, is somewhat younger. He's* ***OLIVE***'*s equal in negativity.* ***OLIVE*** *becomes distracted by something she sees in the mirror.)*

WENDY. I feel like I'm brokering a Mid-East treaty.

ROBERT. We're both very glad to be making this first step. Aren't we, Trey?

TREY. Greatest fantasy come true.

WENDY. Come in, sit down.

ROBERT. Such a different lay-out than ours.

TREY. No, it's the same. This is what our place would look like if we did nothing to it.

WENDY. I know you've seen each other in the hall but I'd like to officially introduce you to Olive.

ROBERT. I'm Robert and this is Trey.

(**OLIVE** *is still pre-occupied with the reflection in the mirror.*)

WENDY. Olive, this is Robert and Trey?

TREY. Is she all right?

OLIVE. *(returning to them)* Yes, she's all right. You're Robert and Trey. I got it.

WENDY. You seemed distracted by something.

OLIVE. So now we're supposed to be all warm and runny like cheddar cheese, your favorite; the smell of which consistently permeates my wall.

WENDY. We really appreciate you coming over like this.

ROBERT. *(almost mesmerized)* What a beautiful mirror? A family heirloom?

TREY. Robert, it's a repro. *(to* **OLIVE***)* Ethan Allen?

OLIVE. *(defensively)* Sears.

TREY. It's just that Robert is extremely knowledgeable about antiques. I mean, the man could be an appraiser for Sotheby's.

ROBERT. There's something very special about it. Wonderful how you can see into the mirror on the opposing wall.

WENDY. How long have you guys lived in the building?

ROBERT. We've *lived* in the building for twelve years –.

OLIVE. What nonsense is that? Irma Sonkin lived next door to me for three decades until her death a year ago.

TREY. If you'd let Robert finish, you would have heard that we've lived on the other side of the building for twelve years but six months ago we moved to this line. A decision we've bitterly rued.

WENDY. Why'd you move? I don't mean to pry.

ROBERT. We had a two bedroom, but since I've retired as an editor and Trey hasn't been working, we've had to tighten our belts.

TREY. Excuse me. You weren't just an editor. Robert Brannigan's perhaps the most influential editor of children's books, ages four to six, in the history of publishing.

ROBERT. Thank you, but that doesn't pertain to why we sold the apartment.

TREY. It pertains to why I'm currently deemed unemployable as an illustrator. Robert and I were considered very much a team. You probably don't know anything about children's literature but we did the Purple Tugboat series.

WENDY. Yes, I do know those books. My nephew was obsessed with Florence, the purple tugboat. Olive, the windows were her eyes and she had the cutest nose made out of rubber tires.

OLIVE. I get the picture.

TREY. When Robert retired, the perception was that I'd also left the business. It's really ugly out there. Children's literature, like the planet Earth, is rapidly headed for obliteration.

ROBERT. We could have moved but we love this neighborhood. I've always felt that there's a beautiful mystery to it.

OLIVE. Kips Bay? It's not uptown, downtown, or midtown. There's no charm or local color. We have a great abundance of dry cleaners.

ROBERT. And I love this building. I was very involved in the lobby renovation. We're now living in a Tuscan villa. Were you friends with Mrs. Sonkin?

OLIVE. Not friends. She was a most disagreeable woman. I was, however, the one who discovered the body.

WENDY. Really? I didn't know that.

OLIVE. She's putting on an act for you. She's heard this story a million times. No one had seen Mrs. Sonkin for quite awhile and then gradually a terrible rotting stench began permeating my wall. Almost as bad as what I've experienced with you. It took two weeks of complaining before the super got around to unlocking her door and we found Mrs. Sonkin. She was propped up in bed, her eyes wide open. She had been dead for over a month and was in an advanced state of decomposition. There were flies and maggots swarming all over the corpse and the bed.

TREY. Thank you. We bought that bed from the estate.

ROBERT. I'm sorry our habitation has caused you such distress.

WENDY. Hear what he's saying, Olive?

TREY. Robert's not apologizing. He's merely stating that the walls in this building are practically made of tissue paper. Consequently, we haven't appreciated each time you've taken your MALLET and banged on the wall.

OLIVE. It wasn't a mallet. It was the end of my plastic swiffer.

TREY. Call it what you will, Missy. It was both violent and unnecessary. You should know that only a few years ago Robert had major heart surgery.

ROBERT. Trey, please.

TREY. The man was on the operating table for seven hours.

ROBERT. You're embarrassing me.

TREY. He's got a zipper scar down his chest like the front of a Dolce and Gabbana knit. So I don't appreciate you disturbing his rest with your crazy lady antics.

OLIVE. I believe you might be the one suffering from a mental disorder. But I'll take the high road and offer you something to drink.

WENDY. This is great. I feel like we're bonding.

TREY. I think we should go.

ROBERT. If we are to be neighbors, then thank you, Olive. I wouldn't object to a glass of water.

TREY. Robert, please. The elderly aren't great at rinsing out their glasses. You can practically see the E Coli prancing.

ROBERT. Wendy says you're an actress.

OLIVE. I earn a living.

WENDY. Olive was the queen of commercials in the eighties and nineties.

ROBERT. Really?

TREY. Jesus, you're the "Gimme the sausage" lady.

ROBERT. Indeed, you are!

WENDY. The close-ups of your face. The perpetual sneer.

ROBERT. They were classics.

OLIVE. My agent negotiated a buy out. I got totally screwed.

ROBERT. Do you have anything currently running?

OLIVE. I had a national spot for a vaginal cream for seniors. It was yanked off the air by the Conservative Right. Ironic considering how often Republican men have contributed to vaginal dryness.

WENDY. Just a few weeks ago, she shot an episode of Manhattan Coroner.

ROBERT. What do you play? Is it a fun part?

OLIVE. A holocaust survivor. I'm playing older than my years.

WENDY. I was with her on the set and saw her scenes on the monitor. She's incredible.

ROBERT. When will it be on?

WENDY. Next week. I can hardly wait.

ROBERT. I gather you two have known each other a very long time.

WENDY. No. We only met like eight months ago. I'm a theatrical company manager. I handle payroll and contracts, etcetera. I was working on a production of *The House of Bernardo Alba* in Montclair, New Jersey. It was connected to the College. Spanish Tragedy! University theatre! Montclair, New Jersey! You've gotta be kidding. I'M MISS BROADWAY! –

OLIVE. You're pushing, dear.

WENDY. Olive was playing the warm, understanding house-keeper.

OLIVE. The director was a Professor at the college. Thought he was the new Stanislavsky. The final straw was when he insisted I bend over the kettle.

TREY. What's so awful about that?

OLIVE. And fart.

WENDY. By mutual agreement Olive left the production before it opened.

OLIVE. That's it. No more theatre for me.

WENDY. Going back and forth from New Jersey, we really hit it off. Not long after, Olive had two very minor episodes. Disorientation. Double Vision. Unsteady gait. She's fully recovered but I got in the habit of checking in on her.

*(**OLIVE** looks towards the mirror over the sofa. She thinks she sees something again.)*

ROBERT. At first, I assumed you were a relative. A niece or a cousin.

WENDY. As far as I know, Olive doesn't have any family. Olive, are you all right?

OLIVE. I thought I saw something in the mirror.

WENDY. Was it a bug? I keep telling her she needs screens.

OLIVE. *(hestitantly)* Sometimes, I think I see something in the mirror within the mirror.

ROBERT. There's something very special about that mirror.

WENDY. You see something? What do you see?

OLIVE. A figure moving very quickly. Just a glimpse.

WENDY. You've never mentioned this before.

OLIVE. I don't want to be carted out of here in a strait-jacket.

ROBERT. It might just be a floater. I get them sometimes.

TREY. *(fascinated)* Robert, let her talk.

OLIVE. It's a man. I've never seen his face…

TREY. What can you tell us about him?

OLIVE. He's got a long neck, a cowlick and protruding ears…And I think I love him.

 (blackout)

End of Scene

Scene Two

(Late afternoon. **WENDY** *and* **ROBERT** *have gone.*
OLIVE *and* **TREY** *are standing in front of the mirror.*
TREY*'s on his third glass of wine. The bottle and an*
empty clean glass are on the coffee table.)

TREY. *(with great enthusiasm)* I am so totally into this, Olive.
The two mirrors. The cowlick. The jug ears! It's fantas-
tic! I had to come back and find out more.

OLIVE. It's kind of a miracle. And something of a responsibility. I'm the guardian of this spirit.

TREY. I'm so honored that you've taken me into your con-
fidence.

OLIVE. Well, it's been hard keeping it to myself.

TREY. It's just so wild that the ghost is in *your* apartment, of
all people.

OLIVE. And why shouldn't it be in my apartment? What?
I'm not famous enough?

TREY. Because you're – too famous. These paranormal
things usually happen to blind women who run curio
shops. Are you sure you don't want some wine? This is
a great Cabernet.

OLIVE. No, thank you. I should have kept my mouth shut.
All I need is the co-op board having more ammunition
against me.

TREY. I won't say a word. Have you thought about having
your agent contact the SciFi Channel?

OLIVE. NO! Now stop it. You're getting carried away
because you're unemployed and bored out of your
skull.

TREY. Well, this is the most exciting thing that's happened
to me for a very long time.

OLIVE. It didn't happen to you. It happened to me. He's
mine and nobody else's

TREY. That's why I want to know more about you. What is
it about the sausage lady that brings forth spirits from
an astral plane?

OLIVE. You're a little wackadoodle. Would I see him better if I moved that mirror slightly to the right? *(She moves towards the non-decorative mirror.)*

TREY. One can't be literal-minded when dealing with the metaphysical.

OLIVE. His name is Howard.

TREY. You're on a first name basis?

OLIVE. I don't engage in conversation with him. I'm not a nutcase.

TREY. Then how do you know his name is Howard?

OLIVE. I just know.

TREY. Does he have a last name?

OLIVE. Only his first name came into my head.

TREY. He's in the vapor.

OLIVE. *(matching his rhythm)* He's in real estate. Verbalizing makes it sound so ludicrous.

TREY. *(excited)* Hey, I once knew a Howard. He died in a hot tub. Performed in drag on weekends.

OLIVE. My Howard is not a transvestite. I don't like where this conversation is heading. In fact, I hate it.

TREY. So you want me to leave?

OLIVE. Did I say I wanted you to leave? You're so prickly. For the record, don't think I'm in any way homophobic. I'm very gay friendly. It's just that I'm slowly getting a picture of who Howard might be. And I don't want anything to muddy it up. So keep your notions to yourself. You can pour me a little bit of that wine. Just a sip.

*(**TREY** pours some wine into her glass.)*

OLIVE. That's too much.

TREY. Look, I'm sure it wasn't the same person. I met this guy years ago in Key West.

OLIVE. Howard lived in Key West.

TREY. How do you know?

OLIVE. I just know.

TREY. And you love him?

OLIVE. Disregard that previous statement.

TREY. Were you ever married?

OLIVE. Uh huh. And divorced for over thirty years. Is all this helping you figure out why I'm the chosen one?

TREY. I'm still filling in the details. Are you friendly with your ex?

OLIVE. No. He married the woman with whom he betrayed me. My husband had a music school in Yonkers. I was the bookkeeper. Among his faculty was a lonely widow, who specialized in the oboe. *(She mimes blowing into the instrument.)* Need I say more?

(The doorbell rings.)

This could be the super.

TREY. Why do you need the super?

OLIVE. A million things. I'm always ignored. At this point, every foot of this joint is Gerry-rigged.

(She opens the door. It's a dignified, ebullient man in his seventies, **SYLVAN GUZICK.***)*

SYLVAN. Mrs. Fisher?

OLIVE. You're not the super.

SYLVAN. No, I'm not the super. Sylvan Guzick. My daughter is the board President, Carol Kandel.

OLIVE. She sent her father? She can't face me herself?

SYLVAN. Are you gonna make me stand in the hall like a Jehovah's Witness?

OLIVE. I'm not sure how I want to handle this situation.

SYLVAN. It's not a situation. Look. I'm coming in. *(He enters the apartment. He immediately sees the decorative mirror and is startled.)* Oy gevalte! That strange old man! Oh, it's a mirror. *(He sees* **TREY.***)* Hello. Sylvan Guzick.

TREY. Trey Chamblay. I live next door.

SYLVAN. Lovely to meet you, Mrs. Fisher. I understand this morning you had a contretemps with my daughter.

OLIVE. Is that what she called it?

SYLVAN. She used stronger language. That's why I'm here. To apologize for her behavior.

OLIVE. Well, this is a first.

TREY. I adore Carol. She's so chic. Do you two need to be alone? I can go.

SYLVAN. No, please. I won't be long. I don't even live here. I'm visiting from Buenos Aires.

OLIVE. Buenos Aires?

SYLVAN. I should be from Boca? Buenos Aires is paradise on earth for retirees. Cosmopolitan, welcoming and you can live like a Czar in a two-bedroom condo on a fixed income. As per your problems in this building, I love my daughter Carol. A wonderful girl, but she can be tough. She takes her role as board President very seriously.

OLIVE. She's struts around like Boss Tweed. She makes me feel like a guttersnipe in Buckingham Palace.

SYLVAN. She can be persnickety about her living quarters. You have to understand, her mother died when she was very young and I remarried and was widowed twice afterwards. Her life was full of constant upheaval.

TREY. Wait. You've been widowed three times. That's terrible.

OLIVE. I don't mean to be offensive, but there's something a little creepy about it.

SYLVAN. I'm not a serial killer. I've lost two wives to cancer and my last wife to heart disease only last year. I loved each of them dearly, and all could be deemed volatile. My life today is peaceful to be sure, but I frankly miss the sturm and drang.

OLIVE. Well, don't come sniffing around here. I've no intention of becoming Bluebeard's fourth wife.

SYLVAN. I'll take due note. So what was the *fracas (pronounced "fra- ah")* this morning between you and Carol?

OLIVE. I was simply telling your daughter about my horrible next door neighbors and not only did I receive no sympathy, she was downright abusive.

SYLVAN. *(to* **TREY***)* You live on this floor. Is it dreadful for you too?

TREY. I'm the horrible neighbor.

OLIVE. You see? I'm not the harridan your daughter and the rest of this building paint me as.

TREY. We're calmly discussing the ghost in Olive's mirror.

OLIVE. DAMN IT, TREY!

SYLVAN. You have a ghost?

OLIVE. No, I do not have a ghost. I don't know what the hell he's talking about.

TREY. I'm sorry. I must have misunderstood you.

SYLVAN. If you're interested in ghosts, my daughter Carol has, for quite a few years, organized through her Temple on Thirty-Fifth Street, tours of haunted synagogues in the tri-state area.

TREY. I had no idea. How cool is that?

SYLVAN. I could never go because of my lingerie business, and then I retired with my wife to South America. But now I'm a free agent. Olive, may I call you Olive? We should join Carol the next time around. You could get to know her better.

TREY. Olive, do you belong to that Temple on Thirty-Fifth Street?

OLIVE. What? You assume I'm Jewish?

TREY. You're not?

OLIVE. I come off pushy and aggressive?

TREY. No.

OLIVE. Because I detect a subtle tinge of anti-Semitism.

SYLVAN. It was an innocent question.

OLIVE. Open to interpretation.

TREY. I will not be accused of being prejudiced.

SYLVAN. Carol loves the theatre. She's written several unproduced plays.

OLIVE. Fisher isn't necessarily a Jewish name.

SYLVAN. Perhaps one evening, the three of us could go…

TREY. I know. So Fisher's your maiden name?

OLIVE. No. I retained my husband's name after the divorce.

TREY. What's your maiden name?

OLIVE. *(simply)* Blechman. Olive Blechman.

SYLVAN. That's not Jewish?

OLIVE. This topic is terminated.

TREY. When I was growing up in Indiana, I was best friends with the one Jewish kid in my class. We were the town misfits. Known to all as the cocksucker and the hebe. I loved having Passover at the Rabkins. It was so theatrical. The symbolic dishes. Reading the Haggadah. You know, Passover is coming up this week. Are you gonna do anything?

OLIVE. I haven't observed Passover in years.

SYLVAN. My daughter has a very grand Seder. Catered, rehearsed and with a theme. I'm not looking forward to it.

TREY. Should we have a Seder?

OLIVE. You've gotta be kidding. You've got to make a brisket. It's an enormous undertaking.

TREY. Forget it. I don't know what I was thinking.

SYLVAN. You kids give up easily. You preheat your oven to 350. Salt and pepper the meat, place it in a roasting pan and let it sit for a couple of hours. How difficult can it be?

OLIVE. It's the whole thing. I detest holidays of any kind.

TREY. It's nice giving and receiving presents. When I was working, I must say I enjoyed the tradition of the Secret Santa.

SYLVAN. Oh, the Secret Santa. I forgot all about that. I used to enjoy doing that with the people who worked for me.

OLIVE. The Secret Santa? What kind of sick people are you? The last time I participated in that disgusting ritual was when I was doing an Odets play in Cleveland five years ago. For the first time in my career, I felt a genuine sense of family with this company. After the final matinee before Christmas, the whole cast and crew gathered in the green room and we exchanged our ten dollar presents. People were getting really nice things; a jar of gourmet roasted peppers, an expensive fashion magazine. I gave the ingénue a lovely box of note cards. My secret Santa was the young man running the lights. I pull off the ribbon, tear off the pretty wrapping paper, open the box, remove the colorful tissue paper, and what do I find but a small, dried dog turd. A canine bowel movement scooped up off the street. *(Reliving the painful betrayal, it builds and builds)* He thought it was funny. The girl playing my daughter doubled over with laughter. The actor playing my son was holding his ribs, he was guffawing so hard. The entire cast. the stage manager, the dressers, the prop crew. All heaving with laughter. I never spoke another word to anyone associated with the production for the rest of the run. So much for Secret Santa. So much for the holiday spirit. So much for stinking humanity.

TREY. Wow. You're Sweeney Todd.

SYLVAN. *(dazzled)* You're wonderful.

(**OLIVE** *sees something moving in the mirror within the mirror. She appears to be receiving a message. Is Howard somehow suggesting she have a Passover Seder?*)

TREY. Come to think of it, I've never gotten a present I really loved. Most of the time, people give you things just to shut you up. So you'll stop crying. So you'll forgive them. So you won't cause any more trouble.

OLIVE. I'll do Passover.

SYLVAN. Is that an invitation?

OLIVE. *(perplexed)* Yeah…I guess it is.

End of Scene

Scene Three

(A few nights later. In the middle of the room is a linen covered card table with four chairs. **ROBERT** *is setting the table, and speaking to* **OLIVE***, who's in the kitchen.)*

ROBERT. This is a very attractive gravy boat. Olive, do you know, in Philadelphia there's a marvelous little shop near Rittenhouse Square that only sells gravy boats? In every conceivable china pattern. Can you hear me?

*(***ROBERT*** quickly crosses to the decorative mirror.)*

We've only a few seconds. Olive's in the kitchen. Trey's in the bathroom. Are you there? I'm not a kook. I'm an extremely rational fellow, with no spiritual beliefs, no interest in the occult. But my heart skipped a beat when I first looked into this mirror. And after you've had heart surgery, believe me, you listen to that organ like an emergency broadcast system. Now this may sound really off the wall, but when this apartment house was first built in the forties, this apartment and ours was one unit. Is it possible, whoever you are, that you were looking for me but got the wrong apartment? *(vulnerably)* Are you someone – who loved me? Follow me next door and we can figure this thing out at our leisure. We have a lovely mirror. Venetian glass. What would you want from me? Total honesty? That would be a blessing.

*(***TREY*** comes out of the bathroom.)*

TREY. Who were you talking to? The man in the mirror?

ROBERT. No. Olive. She kicked me out of the kitchen.

TREY. *(suspiciously)* Is that so? You're not seeing anything *special* in the mirror?

ROBERT. Should I be seeing something special in the mirror? Have you gotten a peek at Olive's secret friend? You've been here quite a bit the last few days.

TREY. If I'm here, darling, it's because I've been working my tits off organizing this Seder. I got Madame's oven repaired. I ordered the brisket. Went all over town today trying to round up Haggadah booklets with some visual flair. I ended up at Park Avenue Judaica, where I found these very stylish mid-century modern Seder booklets. I'm taking them off the shelf, when this woman next to me violently snatches them out of my hand. She had a kid with her. So she says, "My daughter had her eye on these." Really? A five year-old in love with clean lines? And of course, they had nothing left in stock. The salesgirl refused to get involved and let this woman get away with this shit. And then had the audacity to ask *me* to leave the shop. Needless to say, I'm going back tomorrow when the manager is in. Oh yeah.

ROBERT. Trey, is it really necessary to report that salesgirl to her boss?

TREY. She was horrible to me.

ROBERT. Perhaps she was. Maybe she was having a bad day. Maybe her best friend was kidnapped by pirates while on a cruise. Maybe she had a bad canker sore.

TREY. Maybe. Maybe. Maybe. This is so typical.

ROBERT. Typical of what?

TREY. This OCD habit you have of seeing both sides to everything.

ROBERT. That's bad?

TREY. In life, Robert, some things are right and some things are wrong. They just are. When I get into an altercation with a waiter or a receptionist or a salesperson or a hotel concierge or an acupuncturist or a life coach, I demand one hundred percent sympathy from my partner. Okay? I'm not looking for an objective analysis of the situation.

ROBERT. But you get into these altercations every day.

TREY. Once and for all, I do not have rage issues.

ROBERT. I'm not saying that. I've never said that.

TREY. But you think I create these situations.

ROBERT. I think for reasons stemming from your child-hood, you're extremely sensitive to a slight.

TREY. I'm a reactive personality. In my entire life, I've never started an argument.

(**TREY** *accidentally catches a glimpse of himself in the decorative mirror and instinctively smiles and greets his reflection as if he were an old friend.*)

TREY. Hello.

ROBERT. Do you see the man in the mirror?

TREY. Just my reflection. I swear I look ten years younger in this mirror. Maybe not ten years. But my eyes don't look so beady and suspicious. They were beautiful eyes, weren't they? Everyone said so. Wide open, trusting, luminous orphan eyes. Why can't I look like this all the time?

ROBERT. I'll tell you what. For your birthday, I'll pay for you to get your eyes done. Would you like that?

TREY. You'd do that? Really? It ain't cheap.

ROBERT. We won't take a big vacation. You're miserable traveling anyway. I just want you to be happy.

TREY. So the little dump truck had his bags removed, joy reigned throughout the junkyard and they all lived happily ever after. Give up, honey.

(**OLIVE** *enters carrying a few small dishes.*)

OLIVE. What are you boys gabbing about?

TREY. I was commenting that one would never guess this was the apartment of an actress.

OLIVE. I should have a velvet divan and a spot lit portrait of myself?

TREY. I meant, it's an apartment of a woman of many interests.

OLIVE. It's the apartment of a former bookkeeper from Yonkers. We should start the Seder soon. What's keeping the Merry Widower? He should be here by now.

ROBERT. Trey said he was a charming fellow.

OLIVE. The jury is still out. Trey, would you help me set the small dishes?

TREY. Of course. Be nice to Robert. We want him to fall in love with the Seder.

(He goes into the kitchen.)

ROBERT. What are these? Are they a holiday symbol of something wonderful?

OLIVE. The Haroset is a mixture of apples, nuts, wine and spices. It symbolizes the mortar the enslaved Jews made for the torturous building of the Pyramids. And the Zeroa is symbolic of the lamb slaughtered as a Passover sacrifice.

*(**TREY** comes out with two more dishes.)*

ROBERT. A hard boiled egg and a dish of parsley. Does this symbolize birth and renewal?

*(**TREY** returns to the kitchen.)*

OLIVE. The hard boiled egg is the food of mourning. The parsley is dipped in salt water to represent the misery and tears of the Jewish people.

*(**TREY** comes out with two more dishes.)*

ROBERT. Horseradish and this other one just looks like water. Isn't water usually a symbol of hope? And the horseradish certainly is a bright cheerful color.

OLIVE. The horseradish is the Maror, a bitter herb that symbolizes the agony of the enslaved Israelites. *(sincerely and with no irony)* I forgot how much I enjoyed this holiday.

(blackout)

*(Lights up and **OLIVE**, **ROBERT**, **TREY** and **SYLVAN** are in the living room area having drinks.)*

OLIVE. So you're led to believe I bumped off the kid but the twist ending is that the boy's father did it. Okay. Now you don't have to watch.

SYLVAN. I wouldn't miss it for the world.

TREY. Not every day you see the "gimme the sausage" lady in a meaty role.

OLIVE. Very amusing. Enough about show business. I honestly can't remember the last time I had anyone over for dinner.

SYLVAN. Everything smells delicious.

ROBERT. Was your wife a good cook?

OLIVE. Which one?

ROBERT. Your most recent.

SYLVAN. The worst. It was a crime what that woman could do to a chicken tender. Seriously, no joke. I once threw out a vertebrae from chewing on her Beef Wellington. I know I sound disloyal, but she had a great sense of humor about it. Consequently, we ate most of our meals out.

OLIVE. When I was married, I took my cooking very seriously. Every night a three course gourmet dinner for the shmuck.

ROBERT. I love to cook. But Trey also knows his way around the kitchen.

TREY. It's a wonder I do. It's Robert's kitchen. He put the whole thing together, down to the very last dish towel. He collects them you know, from all over the world. You've never seen so many goddam dish towels. But I am definitely the better chef.

ROBERT. Indeed he is. Italian. French. Chinese. Just don't ask him for anything after that fourth glass of wine. Even boiling water becomes an ordeal.

TREY. That wasn't very nice.

ROBERT. I exaggerate. He knows where to draw the line.

TREY. When we met, I was barely out of my teens, and just to be sociable, I would nurse a sloe gin fizz for three hours. Robert *learned* me the pleasures of the extended cocktail hour.

ROBERT. As beautiful as he was, he was insecure about his lack of formal education. A few drinks helped him combat his shyness.

TREY. I came to New York straight out of high school. Was I ever a rube! Robert educated me on wines and food and music. Sent me to art school. I was his Eliza Doolittle.

ROBERT. He makes it sound like a May/December romance. It was more like May/June.

TREY. Robert was still in his twenties, but he was already extremely successful. I had to endure plenty of digs from his sophisticated circle of friends. There were those I won't mention, who called me to my face "a gold-digging, syphilitic whore."

ROBERT. Who said that?

TREY. I don't want to ruin any of your long standing friend-ships.

ROBERT. Who would say something like that?

TREY. Darling, I'm not gonna tell you. But you went to college with him and he lives on East Fifty-Fourth Street. Believe me, I put up with a lot. The snubs. The humiliations. And even after a thirty year, Caldecott Award-winning career, I'm still dismissed in certain quarters as a beautiful but untalented whore.

SYLVAN. My friend, you suffer from low self-esteem. Here's an exercise. Come up with one word that people would use to define you. One word.

TREY. *(immediately)* Whore.

SYLVAN. This isn't working. Look. It's never too late to start anew. In fact, I decided today that I'm going back to school. I want to study computer Photoshop. I've been fiddling around manipulating old family photographs. Giving them different colors and backgrounds. I want to learn more about it.

ROBERT. Trey does beautiful things on the computer. I'm sure he could give you some tips.

TREY. *(focused on his drink)* Any time.

OLIVE. Sylvan, you're not going back to school.

SYLVAN. What do you mean?

OLIVE. That's one of those ideas that come and go. And if you do enroll, ten to one you end up dropping out.

SYLVAN. I don't think so. I'm the type that follows through.

OLIVE. Even so. How many photographs are you gonna retouch? Two or three? Then you lose interest and tossed away good money.

SYLVAN. I don't think so. I do a lot of crafts. Gluing shells on picture frames. Trimming lamp shades. I'm mad for decoupage.

OLIVE. You'll see I'm right. You'll regret it.

(SYLVAN *laughs heartily.*)

What's so funny?

SYLVAN. You're just a little bully, aren't you? Olive, I toast you. I enjoy a provocateur or should I say, a provocateuse.

(SYLVAN *drinks in her honor.* OLIVE, *unsettled that she wasn't able to undermine his enthusiasm, decides to get things moving.*)

OLIVE. It's time we start reading the Haggadah. Shall we go to the table?

(OLIVE, TREY, *and* ROBERT *move over to the table.* OLIVE *takes a match out of a box of kitchen matches and lights the candles.*)

ROBERT. It's too bad Wendy can't be with us.

OLIVE. Just as well. The way she performs for the two of you, every time she opens her mouth, it's open mike night at the Gay and Lesbian Center.

TREY. I think she's fun.

OLIVE. She had some sort of dinner date. She'll join us for dessert.

ROBERT. I'm looking forward to a wonderful, new experience.

OLIVE. Before we begin, I just want to say, I'm glad you've risked entering the lions' den and are with me tonight for Pesach. And thank you, Trey, for helping me get this all together.

TREY. My pleasure.

ROBERT. This is not only Passover but Armistice Day.

SYLVAN. L'chaim.

ALL. L'chaim.

TREY. Well, I'm totally in the mood to read the entire Haggadah.

OLIVE. My angel, we'd be sitting here all night.

TREY. Yes, but it's beautiful.

OLIVE. It's endless.

SYLVAN. Olive has a point. I don't know any family, except the most Orthodox, who read the entire thing.

OLIVE. Tovah Feldshuh doesn't read the whole thing.

TREY. I want Robert to hear it. I love showing him new things. He's the best audience in the world.

ROBERT. That's very sweet of you, Trey, but it's all right.

TREY. No, Robert, I want you to hear it.

OLIVE. Let's not get into a snit about this.

TREY. Who's in a snit?

OLIVE. We'll do the abbreviated Haggadah. Sylvan, do you read Hebrew?

SYLVAN. Some. You want me to read the opening blessing?

OLIVE. Please.

SYLVAN. *(reading)*
Barukh atah Adonai, Eloheinu melekh ha'alam
Asher kidishanu b'mitz'votav v'tzivanu
Ner shel Shabbat v'shel Yom Tov.

ALL. Amen.

(**OLIVE** *picks up a piece of matzoh.*)

ROBERT. We all get to read?

OLIVE. We go around the table, each taking turns reading a passage.

ROBERT. Like a parlor game. I love it.

OLIVE. "This is the bread of affliction that our fathers ate in the land of Egypt. Whoever is hungry, let him come and eat." Blah, blah, blah, blah.

TREY. What's with the blah, blah, blah?

OLIVE. It's just repetition. *(reading)* "This year we are here; next year in Jerusalem." I was offered an Israeli tour of *Fiddler* playing Yente. For the money they were paying, I wouldn't go to Ogunquit let alone Jaifa. Blah, blah, blah, blah. "Next year we will be free people." Enough with the Matzoh. The second cup of wine is poured. *(They all drink.)* In this next part, a child asks the first of the four questions. Sylvan, you be the child.

SYLVAN. "Why is this night different from all other nights?"

OLIVE. "On all other nights we need not dip even once, on this night we do so twice." Skip to the next big paragraph. Your turn, Robert.

ROBERT. *(reading fast and with little inflection)* "We were slaves to Pharaoh in Egypt, and the Lord, our God, took us out from here with a strong hand and an outstretched arm. If the Holy one had not taken our fathers out of Egypt-

OLIVE. You have a bus to catch? I can't understand a thing you're saying.

TREY. Maybe you need to get your hearing checked.

OLIVE. Maybe you should stop being a wise ass and read the next passage.

SYLVAN. Maybe you should both behave.

TREY. *(reading in a very theatrical and expressive voice)* "It happened that Rabbi Eliezer, Rabbi Yehoshua, Rabbi Elazar ben Azaryah, Rabbi Akiva and Rabbi Tarphon were reclining at a seder in B'nei Berak. They were discussing the exodus from Egypt all that night, until their students came and told them –

OLIVE. Don't read in that phony voice.

TREY. I'm not reading in a phony voice.

SYLVAN. I found it very effective.

OLIVE. He's reading like Joan Crawford. Just speak like a normal person.

TREY. "—until their students came and told them; *(with rising intensity)* "Our Masters! The time has come for reciting the morning Shema!"

OLIVE. Oh, come on. That's too much.

TREY. Do you see the exclamation point after "Shema"? An exclamation point indicates "with emphasis."

OLIVE. Oh my, I didn't realize I was dealing with a member of the Old Vic.

TREY. I didn't realize you were now functioning as director.

ROBERT. Trey's merely being enthusiastic.

SYLVAN. He's giving it a sense of drama.

OLIVE. He's making a camp travesty of a holy ritual.

TREY. You're the one making this Seder a travesty with your constant interruptions, editing and criticism.

OLIVE. Are you through?

TREY. Yes, I'm through.

OLIVE. Then I'm gonna read the second question. "When will this fucking night ever end?"

(blackout)

(Lights up. They are eating the brisket in stony silence. The front door opens and **WENDY** *arrives, breathlessly. She throws off her coat.)*

WENDY. I'm so sorry I'm late.

OLIVE. You said you were going to be late.

TREY. *(pointedly)* Where ever you were, I hope *you* were having a good time.

WENDY. Hello. I'm Wendy. You must be Sylvan.

SYLVAN. You haven't arrived a moment too soon. Did you have a pleasant evening?

WENDY. It was a business dinner and I've been very insecure. Doubting myself.

*(***WENDY*** *checks herself in the mirror.)*

(distressed) My hair. *(likes what she sees)* Doesn't look too bad. I tell ya, there really is something about this mirror, Olive. I look in it and suddenly I feel I have stature and substance, like the portrait of George Washington by Gilbert Stuart. Only hot and appealing. So how was my evening? Well, I dined with this

guy from LA. He's with the Screen Actors Guild and they're considering me for an important position with the union. P.S. He's gay. Bodes well.

OLIVE. This is a new one. Not a word was ever mentioned.

WENDY. I didn't want to jinx it by talking about it too much.

(**SYLVAN** *gives her his seat.*)

SYLVAN. You sit here.

(**WENDY** *sits in* **SYLVAN**'s *seat. He takes his plate and sits nearby in the desk chair.*)

ROBERT. You'd be moving to Los Angeles?

WENDY. If I get it. They'd want me to start immediately.

(*It's clear by* **OLIVE**'s *grim expression and silence, that's she's not too pleased about this.*)

ROBERT. How do you feel about that?

WENDY. Excited. Tantalized. But the idea of starting all over in a strange city. Oh boy.

TREY. Good jobs are hard to come by. You're looking at a gentleman of enforced leisure.

ROBERT. Well, this is one New Yorker who's no L.A. basher. I love the weather. The dry heat, then the way it cools down in the evening.

SYLVAN. I'm with you, pal. The palm trees. The smell of the Jacaranda. Olive, you spend much time in Los Angeles?

OLIVE. No. My work in television and film was mostly in New York. Pass the yams.

WENDY. I love Seders. This afternoon, I was actually reading the Passover service on my new kindle.

SYLVAN. Kindle. It sounds like one of Tevye's daughters.

WENDY. I say this without exaggeration; it is my great sorrow that I was not born a Jew. Tortured, scorned, exiled, exterminated. I have always felt the weight of their two thousand years of oppression.

OLIVE. What the hell have you been smoking?

WENDY. I'm just saying, I feel in my heart of hearts that I am a Jewess.

OLIVE. You were born a Catholic. Enjoy being a Catholic.

WENDY. Ever since I was a kid and saw the movie *The Ten Commandments*, I've identified with the plight of the Jews. Over the years, I've put in many hours of volunteer work for Jewish charities. My refrigerator is stocked with Jewish foods.

OLIVE. So why haven't you converted?

WENDY. I'm not an electrical switch plate. I don't have to undergo some sort of conversion to feel what I feel.

SYLVAN. She enjoys whitefish and chopped liver. Don't call the police.

OLIVE. If it means so much to you to be a Jew, you take the courses at the Shul and you become officially Jewish.

WENDY. Why are you making such a big megillah over this?

OLIVE. Because it's silly. And even a tad offensive.

TREY. If she wants to be a Jew, for Christ's sake, let her be a Jew.

ROBERT. Our Little Purple Tugboat series touched on this issue. Flo was ridiculed and ostracized by the other skiffs, sailboats and yachts in the harbor. And yet when push came to shove, that little tugboat, with her purple paint peeling, and her two big windows splashed with rain, had the strength and courage to pull a large ship into port during a horrendous storm.

OLIVE. What madness are you jabbering about?

ROBERT. I'm talking about compassion and tolerance.

TREY. All peoples should be respected.

OLIVE. That's a dumb thing to say.

ROBERT. Don't call him dumb.

OLIVE. The conversation around this table is crazy talk.

TREY. What was so crazy about what I said? All people deserve respect? That's such a dumb thing to say?

OLIVE. Not all people deserve respect. Bigots, racists, child abusers. None of them deserve my respect.

TREY. *(mildly sloshed)* I meant Jews, Gentiles…*(fumbling)* the Cherokee. I personally represent several minorities that are unfairly prosecu—persecuted.

OLIVE. Seriously, I'd like to know what persecuted minority other than gay you represent.

TREY. *(slurring his words)* Let's just say, it's not easy living in New York City if you don't toe the official political party line.

SYLVAN. *(whispering to **ROBERT**)* He shouldn't drink any more.

ROBERT. It's all right.

OLIVE. The party line? What party line?

TREY. If you're not Miss Liberal Democrat, forget it.

OLIVE. Next you're gonna tell me you're a Republican. That would be the perfect capper to this rotten evening.

ROBERT. Trey's family is very conservative.

OLIVE. *(disbelieving)* Trey, did you vote Republican in the last Presidential election?

TREY. Once you pull the curtain closed, it's a private… thing.

WENDY. Shall we read about the ten plagues?

SYLVAN. What page, dear?

OLIVE. Well, who did you vote for?

TREY. That's a complicated question.

OLIVE. I'd say it's a very simple question.

ROBERT. Trey doesn't have to answer anything.

WENDY. *(reading)* "It is said that the Holy One set against the Egyptians his full anger, fury –."

OLIVE. *(relentlessly)* Wendy, cool it. This is my table and I want to know how you voted in the last election?

TREY. I'm a fiscal Republican. I have strong concerns about the financial security of this country.

OLIVE. But you're gay. That's like me, a Jew, voting for Eichmann. You vote for someone who doesn't want you to exist?

SYLVAN. Perhaps you're more of a Libertarian.

TREY. I have concerns beyond gay rights. I have a much wider view of the world.

OLIVE. Your view is ridiculous.

ROBERT. We may not all agree with his politics but it's his right to express them.

OLIVE. How do you sleep at night? You've betrayed your own tribe.

TREY. I don't have to take this.

ROBERT. You *don't* have to take this.

TREY. Thank you, Robert, for once being a hundred per cent on my side.

ROBERT. You didn't come here to be insulted.

WENDY. How many of the four questions have you asked?

OLIVE. *(to* **WENDY***)* Three and here's the fourth. "Why don't you stick your head in the toilet?"

ROBERT. We're going.

(**ROBERT** *and* **TREY** *get up from the table.)*

WENDY. *(cheerfully)* I didn't take it personally.

SYLVAN. Everyone, come back to the table. I brought a gorgeous cinnamon apple farfel kugel.

OLIVE. The cuddly, Jewish grandpa schtick. I find it cloying.

SYLVAN. *(stands up)* To hell with the kugel. You don't talk to guests like that. You don't talk to me like that.

OLIVE. Guzick, like it or lump it.

(**ROBERT** *and* **TREY** *have almost reached the front door.* **OLIVE** *follows them.)*

Trey, the only way I can reconcile your voting Republican is that you're a sad, self-hating homosexual.

TREY. No. I'm just a homosexual who hates you.

OLIVE. Sincerely, you need psychiatric help.

TREY. I wonder what a shrink would say about an old woman who has a gay real estate agent stuck in her mirror.

OLIVE. Go on and try to humiliate me. Join the thousands who've succeeded.

ROBERT. Trey, I'm leaving.

TREY. You recall our hostess revealed that she sees a man in the mirror within her mirror. She didn't tell you that his name is Howard and coincidentally, you and I met him in Key West years ago. Remember, at Kevin's Halloween party, he came as Phyllis Diller?

OLIVE. Shut up. Just shut up!

TREY. I'm sorry. I forgot that you want to keep him to yourself.

ROBERT. Her ghost is Howard?

SYLVAN. What's going on here?

WENDY. Oh, my God. Oh my God. Howard is my brother!

END OF ACT ONE

ACT TWO

Scene One

*(A few days later. The doorbell rings. **OLIVE** comes out of the bedroom, putting on her coat. There's a new spring in her step. She answers the door. It's **WENDY**.)*

OLIVE. Darling, love the skirt. Very becoming. Thanks for stopping by but I've got that appointment at one thirty with the podiatrist.

WENDY. I know. That's why I'm here. To accompany you.

OLIVE. I forgot you said you'd do that. I'd really like to go alone.

WENDY. You're mad at me.

OLIVE. I'm not mad. I just want to go alone. It looks like a nice day out.

WENDY. I'll walk you halfway. And we can discuss what happened at the Seder.

OLIVE. What do you mean, what happened?

WENDY. Well, you know, that the man in your mirror happens to be my brother. That's kind of a big deal.

OLIVE. I see it more as a jolly coincidence.

WENDY. Olive, I have unresolved issues with my brother. Your mirror could bring about the peace of mind that has so long eluded me.

OLIVE. Wendy, the most amazing thing has happened!

WENDY. My brother has risen from the dead.

OLIVE. *(with uncharacteristic glee)* My picture is in *The Times* today.

WENDY. What?

OLIVE. My picture is in *The Times.* I never thought this would happen, unless it was accompanied by an obituary.

WENDY. Why is your picture in *The Times*? Did they hear you have a ghost in your mirror?

OLIVE. The TV listings. They ran a photo of me from my Manhattan Coroner episode. It's on tonight.

WENDY. That's wonderful. Olive, if I could just spend some quality time with your mirror.

OLIVE. Here let me read this to you. *(She picks up the newspaper.)* "A holocaust survivor is the prime suspect in the slaying of a teen age Neo-Nazi gang member. Olive Fisher guest stars." Guest stars. Can you believe that? I wasn't contracted to have that kind of billing.

WENDY. You had a very big part. Olive, that mirror holds the key to—

OLIVE. And a picture? You have to understand, Wendy, big names receive that sort of attention from an episodic. *The Times* had to get this from a press release. Is it possible that the producers are positioning me for an Emmy nomination?

WENDY. Is that how it works?

OLIVE. In this business, one can't assume or predict anything. I've been getting calls all morning. People I haven't heard from in ages saw the picture in the paper and are so happy for me.

WENDY. And wait till they see your performance. Remember, I was there.

OLIVE. I was good. Wasn't I?

WENDY. You were more than good. You were devastating.

OLIVE. It was a well written part. I had four great scenes. I was helped by the director. He knew what he was doing.

WENDY. I thought you said he was an untalented fraud.

OLIVE. I groused a little. When I wrapped for the day, I knew he was pleased with me. Does it sound foolish to say I'm feeling a kind of pride? I've earned my living as an actor lo these many years and I've maintained a semblance of integrity, even doing all those silly commercials. I'm not one for patting myself on the back, but a lot of the ideas for the original "Gimme the Sausage" campaign came from me. And today it's considered one of the classic commercials of all time. It's not Ibsen but perhaps it's not something to be dismissed.

WENDY. I'm so glad to hear you say that.

OLIVE. Now this episode is something special. I finally got a chance to show on film that I'm not just an ethnic sight gag, and was allowed to express a range of emotion. Maybe this could lead to other opportunities for dramatic roles. Am I being ridiculous?

WENDY. Not at all.

OLIVE. Strange that this should suddenly happen.

WENDY. How is it strange? You've paid your dues.

OLIVE. I've been searching for some kind of a sign. A dollop of encouragement as I move into the third act of my life. I got it this morning. I knew he wouldn't let me down.

WENDY. He? Who's he?

OLIVE. Did I say "he?'

WENDY. Yeah, you said "he." You meant Howard, didn't you?

OLIVE. No, I did not mean Howard. I meant God. OK?

WENDY. I'm not buying it. You're a confirmed atheist.

OLIVE. I never said that.

WENDY. You've told me numerous times that you've been given the finger by the Jews, the Baptists, the Unitarians, and the B'hai.

OLIVE. All right. All right. This morning in the shower, I received a message…from Howard.

WENDY. You did? Well, what did he say? Did he mention me?

OLIVE. I couldn't hear very well, because of the water pressure. In this building, it's either a fine spray or a painful torrent. The gist as I could figure it out, was that "upon the full moon, all will be revealed." Tonight is the full moon.

WENDY. And all will be revealed. He's gonna make an appearance in the mirror. And not from the back but from the front. We're gonna see his face!

OLIVE. I think it's regarding my TV show tonight and that my talent will finally be revealed to all.

WENDY. Maybe it's both. Howard had a great interest in the entertainment field.

OLIVE. A question that haunts me; Wendy, did you brother ever do drag?

WENDY. He did a pitch perfect Phyllis Diller. But it remained a hobby. He flirted with many careers. I was always very judgmental. The last day of his life we had a terrible fight on the telephone and I hung up on him. Before I could call back and apologize, he had a massive heart attack while soaking in a friend's hot tub. Olive, I need closure. Please, let me come over tonight and watch the show with you.

OLIVE. So you can see Howard?

WENDY. Yes. So I can see Howard. But don't get me wrong, I'd really like to watch the show with you. I feel invested.

OLIVE. I appreciate your candor. The show starts at nine. But no talking. I know how you like to gab and comment on everything.

(The doorbell rings.)

That must be the super. For a month I've been asking him to fix the bedroom window. It's swollen shut. This building would like nothing more than for me to drop dead of heat exhaustion.

*(She answers the door and it's **ROBERT**.)*

Yeah?

ROBERT. I saw the photo in *The Times*. I just had to congratulate you.

OLIVE. Yes, it's very exciting.

ROBERT. Hello, Wendy. May I come in?

OLIVE. I'm on my way to an appointment.

(**ROBERT** *steps all the way into the apartment.*)

ROBERT. That picture was so dramatic.

OLIVE. It's a highly dramatic role.

WENDY. She's got four big scenes.

ROBERT. I already set our TIVO.

OLIVE. *(yielding)* That's very nice of you.

WENDY. Olive has graciously invited me to watch the show with her. And…oh, I've got to say it.

OLIVE. Wendy, please—

WENDY. Olive received a message from Howard that he's going to make an appearance in the mirror tonight during a commercial break.

OLIVE. I never said that. You're embellishing. She's embellishing.

ROBERT. You'll be able to see him? May I join you? For the show and the miracle?

OLIVE. I'm sorry, but no. This is a private affair.

ROBERT. Have I not been completely respectful of the unique properties of this mirror from the moment I walked in here?

OLIVE. Yes, you have. But I really dislike like watching TV with a group. I never go to Oscar parties.

ROBERT. I've got the most marvelous jar of tapenade and some incredible duck liver pate.

OLIVE. All right, you can join us. But you can't bring Trey. He's the type that never shuts up. I guarantee you; he will spoil this night for me. When he drinks, he can be very cutting and sarcastic.

ROBERT. You don't know the real Trey.

OLIVE. I think I do.

ROBERT. You won't believe it, but he can be the most sensitive, caring person. When I was recuperating from my
heart surgery, he was extraordinary. He anticipated my
every need, knew exactly when to be tough with me,
when to shut up.

OLIVE. That I haven't seen.

ROBERT. There were times when I simply needed to be
held. And he did. He saved my life. But if you insist on
not inviting him –

OLIVE. Thank you. I'd rather he not come.

ROBERT. I could say I'm visiting my friend, Clark. Trey
finds him unbearable.

WENDY. We'll be next door. Trey might hear us.

ROBERT. We'll just have to talk very softly. And we could
turn the volume low.

OLIVE. No. We're not turning the volume low. This whole
thing is a terrible idea.

ROBERT. This is what we'll do. We'll keep the volume of the
TV normal. I'll simply say I'm going to Clark's and I'll
leave the apartment and go to the elevator. He'll hear
the elevator door open and close. And if you keep
your door slightly ajar, I can just slip in.

WENDY. That sounds doable.

ROBERT. Oh, but what about the tapenade? How do I get
that out of the apartment?

WENDY. You brought it with you to Clark's.

ROBERT. Clark has a million food phobias. He survives on
nothing but Dipsy Doodles. I can put the tapenade
in a bag but Trey might ask what's in the bag. I can
make sure he sees me packing DVD's and then when
he's not looking, I can go into the kitchen and grab
the tapenade and the liver pate. But what if he has a
sudden craving for tapenade and goes into the fridge
and it's not there. I could go back to the store now
and get something else for us to eat and bring it here
earlier. But he's gonna want to go out this afternoon.
He was hoping we'd go to a movie. I suppose I could
leave him after the movie and tell him I was—

OLIVE. LET HIM COME! I'll put up a notice on the lamp post and invite the entire neighborhood. Maybe this is what Howard wants. Upon the full moon all will be revealed.

End of Scene

Scne Two

(Later that afternoon. **OLIVE** *enters the apartment. She's followed by* **SYLVAN***, who's carrying a large framed mirror. He puts it down.)*

SYLVAN. How the hell did you get this into a cab?

OLIVE. The man in the thrift shop helped me. But when I tried to get it out of the cab, did you notice that neither the super nor the doorman would lift a finger? No one believes I'm being persecuted. I'm like a Tutsis and the co-op board are the Hutu. My biggest regret, and I have many, was not buying this place in '78 when I was offered a low insiders' price.

SYLVAN. How low?

OLIVE. Thirty thousand. At the time, my accountant said it was a risky investment. He should rot in Hell in an overpriced studio.

SYLVAN. Regrets are futile.

OLIVE. Regrets provide fine entertainment when there's nothing on cable. It was a lucky break you happened to be walking in the building when you did. I'm grateful.

SYLVAN. You're obviously gonna need help putting this up. What room is it going in?

OLIVE. This room.

SYLVAN. Three mirrors in one room? I guess it makes it look bigger.

OLIVE. No, it's replacing that mirror.

(She points to a smaller mirror on the wall.)

SYLVAN. Ahhh, that's the mirror in which you see – you know who. Okay. You want me to put it up now?

OLIVE. Thank you. That would be wonderful.

(He lifts the old mirror off the wall and leans it against the desk.)

Do we need to change the picture hook?

SYLVAN. I think the one you have will more than suffice.

(He lifts the new mirror and places it on the hook.)

They don't make mirrors anymore with this glass this thick. Is it straight?

OLIVE. It's tilting to the right. That certainly won't do in this apartment.

SYLVAN. It certainly won't. Olive, I share your passionate liberal beliefs, but you were out of line at Pesach. You don't lash out at people you've invited over for a brisket.

OLIVE. Criticism accepted. I overreacted.

SYLVAN. Many men would not forgive you so quickly. I don't want you looking upon my generosity of spirit as a sign of weakness.

OLIVE. I don't. But you've got to understand, Sylvan. I've been living in this uncharted territory between Third Avenue and the hereafter. It can be very trying.

(OLIVE *looks in the decorative mirror, and thus into the new opposing mirror, attempting to see if this would make her access to Howard any easier.)*

OLIVE. Well, this definitely gives me a better view of his world.

SYLVAN. Is he in there? I make it sound like he's on the toilet. Forgive me. This is none of my affair.

OLIVE. You must think I'm out of my mind.

SYLVAN. I should, but you don't seem like a crazy person.

OLIVE. Maybe I am. You'd like to hear more, wouldn't you? You'd like to hear what a comfort he is? How his mere presence in the mirror seems to set me on the right track? You want me to explain something I'd be the first to dismiss and laugh at in others?

SYLVAN. Olive, I like you. And the more you like someone, the more you respect their privacy.

OLIVE. *(almost childlike)* I don't understand, given my behavior each time we've met, why you like me.

SYLVAN. It must be a deeply ingrained streak of masochism. I'm fascinated by feisty women.

OLIVE. Feisty? I can be impossible.

SYLVAN. I wish I could be a bit more "impossible." I was born with a placid temperament.

OLIVE. That's not a disability.

SYLVAN. It used to drive my mother wild. She used to say I accepted everything too readily, that you could kick me in the ass twenty times and I'd come back for more. She thought it displayed an inherent low expectation of the human race.

OLIVE. I'm sorry but your mother was wrong. You have great empathy for people. It's a sterling quality. Sylvan, come with me to the mirror. *(She gestures towards the decorative mirror.)*

SYLVAN. You don't have to do this.

OLIVE. I want to. Look in the mirror within the mirror.

SYLVAN. I'd rather not.

OLIVE. I got a message from him this morning.

SYLVAN. A message?

OLIVE. He said, "Tonight all will be revealed."

SYLVAN. That's quite a message. I hope it's everything you want it to be.

OLIVE. Look in the mirror.

SYLVAN. Olive, there's nothing in there for me. It's your domain. My magical mirror is probably waiting for me at a flea market at Plaza Dorrego. Anyway, I'd much rather look at you. You're an attractive woman.

OLIVE. Sylvan, you're flirting with me. Nobody's flirted with me since Nixon resigned.

SYLVAN. I hope you enjoyed it.

OLIVE. Nixon's resignation? I got out the good silver.

SYLVAN. I meant my flirting.

OLIVE. I'm not opposed. But it's not gonna get you anywhere. Don't think because I'm an actress, I'm an easy lay.

SYLVAN. You're assuming I'm some kind of a wolf. Maybe I'm a romantic who would prefer to take this in increments. We could test the waters with a simple kiss.

OLIVE. All right. Come here.

(They kiss.)

You're a good kisser. And you have a very appealing masculine scent. You don't overdo it with the after shave.

SYLVAN. Should we sit down on the sofa?

OLIVE. I don't know. You sit and then before you know it, garments come off.

SYLVAN. Let's take the risk and sit.

*(**OLIVE** and **SYLVAN** sit on the sofa; two awkward teenagers.)*

SYLVAN. It's a comfortable couch.

OLIVE. Well worn.

SYLVAN. I wish I could have seen you on the stage.

OLIVE. You make me sound like Lillian Russell.

SYLVAN. I'm looking forward to seeing you on television tonight.

OLIVE. I'm excited by it too. I haven't felt excited about anything in a very long time.

SYLVAN. Maybe that's why you're looking particularly pretty today.

OLIVE. *(enjoying the flirtation)* Here you go again.

SYLVAN. You know, Olive, I have show business in *my* blood. My aunt was a star of the Yiddish Theatre. Ever heard of Bella Maisel?

OLIVE. Of course, I've heard of Bella Maisel. In fact, in the early seventies, for a brief moment, I was in her company. She did a weekend of farewell performances at Town Hall.

SYLVAN. I was at every one of those shows. Who did you play?

OLIVE. A townsperson. I was just starting out. For some reason, Madame Maisel took an instant dislike to me. In front of the entire company, she would mock and ridicule my pronunciation of my one line.

SYLVAN. You know, I was nearly killed that final Sunday matinee. I went backstage after the performance and the stage manager told me to wait for my aunt in the wing. He said she was talking to a member of the cast. I waited and waited and finally the door to her dressing room opened and I moved from my spot. At that very moment, a lighting instrument from high above came crashing to the floor, barely missing me by inches.

OLIVE. I think I was the one she was talking to. I waited till everyone in the company had left, so I could ask Madame to sign my program and to apologize for my terrible line reading. I remember she said, "Today was my farewell performance and it should be yours as well."

SYLVAN. I'm sorry to hear that, but you know, if you hadn't left her dressing room at exactly that moment, I would have remained on that spot and most likely been killed. I owe you my life, Olive Fisher. May I come over tonight and watch your show with you?

OLIVE. *(yielding)* I'd like that. It feels good having you around.

SYLVAN. May I kiss you again?

(He moves in closer. Distracted, **OLIVE** *looks towards the mirror.)*

OLIVE. *(with a haunted sensitivity)* What would happen if I hung the third mirror on that other wall? Would I see more?

*(***SYLVAN*** *is getting the feeling that he may be involved in a romantic triangle.)*

End of Scene

Scene Three

(That night. **WENDY, TREY, ROBERT, SYLVAN** *and* **OLIVE** *are all seated in front of the television. The sound has been turned off. The coffee table is filled with plates of crackers, dip and cheese. The third mirror has replaced a painting on the wall.)*

WENDY. I'm madly in love with this cheese. Where did you get it?

TREY. We belong to a cheese club. It's out of this world. At the first of every month we get in the mail two artisanal cheeses. One domestic. One foreign. In December, you get a third one for free.

ROBERT. Sometimes they come wrapped in linen or chestnut leaves.

TREY. Robert and I get such a kick out of it. You know how some couples love playing golf together? We eat cheese. Honey, I live for the first of the month.

OLIVE. The first of the month? I knew it. That's when the stench is at its worst.

ROBERT. This one is an Epoisses de Bourgogne. You want me to put some on a cracker for you?

OLIVE. No, thank you, I have an aversion to cheese.

SYLVAN. That's terrible. You can't even enjoy a slice of pizza?

OLIVE. I can tolerate a bland mozzarella. Now may we please turn up the volume?

ROBERT. Why? The show's not on yet.

TREY. We'll know when the show is about to start. Look. The previous program is still on.

OLIVE. You're making me extremely nervous. And put down that remote. That's for the DVR.

SYLVAN. Is this it?

OLIVE. That's for the DVD player. That's the one for the TV.

WENDY. Olive, you're still getting it confused. That's the wand for the old VCR. This is the one for the DVD which also controls the VHS, which you don't have anymore. That wand is for the Panasonic in the bedroom. This is for the Toshiba. But the power button is on the Time Warner. Got it?

TREY. Got it. Tonight, I'll be the Vice-President in charge of remotes.

OLIVE. This show is very important to me.

ROBERT. Of course it is. That's why we wanted to watch it with you.

OLIVE. None of you are fooling me. Except for Sylvan, who I believe is genuinely interested in my TV appearance, the rest of you are all here for one reason and one reason only; to take a gander at "he who shall not be named."

WENDY. We are here to witness an extraordinary performance by Olive Fisher and an unbilled guest appearance from my brother Howard.

TREY. I'm very happy for you, Wendy, but personally, I'm kind of over the Howard thing.

OLIVE. Then why are you here?

TREY. Because, I didn't want to be by myself, Meryl Streep of the Sausage Pattie.

SYLVAN. You were lonely. Nothing to be ashamed of. It grabs you when you least expect it. I'll be at the buffet at the Cabeza de Vaca, in Puerto Madero, and some beautiful young couple will be standing in line in front of me, her head resting on his shoulder, and suddenly I'm doubled over with loneliness like I've got an attack of colitis.

OLIVE. Sylvan, you're still in mourning. I think my show's starting.

SYLVAN. No, it isn't. I've been in and out of mourning so many times, I've worn out my black Burberry suit. I'm beginning to feel guilty when I ring a woman's bell, as if I were a *malchah movitz*, the angel of death.

ROBERT. I'm sure that will pass. You seem pretty together.

SYLVAN. Antidepressants. For a year now. I don't come off like a zombie? Because at optimum, I'm not what you'd call "mercurial."

WENDY. Like this Epoisses de Bourgogne, I think you're delicious. All right, guys, since tonight is all about truth telling.

OLIVE. Tonight is not all about truth telling. It's about watching my show in silence. And even though I'm recording it, I wanna watch in real time. Look. It's about to start.

WENDY. No, it isn't. Everyone, I've got big news. I can't hold it in any longer.

TREY. You got the job in L.A.

WENDY. *(overjoyed)* Yes, I got the job!! They called just before I left the house.

SYLVAN. Congratulations.

ROBERT. This is something you really wanted.

WENDY. Absolutely. I'm so excited. It's a very big move.

TREY. Do you know people there?

ROBERT. We have great friends we'd be delighted to connect you with.

TREY. Kyle. Mitzie.

ROBERT. The two Tommys.

TREY. *(to ROBERT)* As soon as we get back to the apartment, let's work the rolodex. *(to WENDY)* Honey, this is us at our best. We love networking our friends and eating cheese.

WENDY. Thank you. My brother had two very close friends who live in Santa Monica. Female impersonators. They said they'd take me under their wing. Olive, I feel so guilty leaving you.

OLIVE. I'm a big girl. But do you really want to go to L.A.? I mean, really? Cause I sense some genuine hesitation.

WENDY. Of course I want to go.

ROBERT. How are you sensing hesitation? She's overjoyed.

OLIVE. I know you're concerned about the driving.

SYLVAN. So she takes a few lessons before she goes. I'll rent a car and take you driving.

WENDY. I'm not that afraid of driving. It's just been awhile.

OLIVE. I'm not trying to influence you one way or another. But have you thought this out? Once you give up a New York apartment, you can never come back.

TREY. That's not true.

OLIVE. It is true. I know what she pays in rent. She'll never get that again. Sylvan talks about loneliness. Loneliness is endemic to Los Angeles. They have one of the highest suicide rates in the country, particularly among older single women in show business.

SYLVAN. Don't do this to her.

OLIVE. I care. Yes, I'm painting a grim picture but, Wendy, I know you. Under the breezy, brassy facade, you're extremely vulnerable. You think I don't listen to you, but I do. You've told me how often you cry alone at night. Multiply that by ten in LA. And don't expect too much from the female impersonators. By profession they're self-centered and imperious. Within weeks, you'll find yourself their handmaiden and at their beck and call.

(**WENDY** *looks totally beaten down.*)

Aaaaahhhh! Turn up the sound! The show's starting!

End of Scene

Scene Four

(An hour later. The group hasn't changed position. We hear the closing lines of the television show.)

CORONER ONE (V.O). Those who forget the past are condemned to repeat it.

CORONER TWO (V.O.). Case closed.

(The familiar dramatic chords signifying the end of the episode are heard. The music over the credits plays. SYLVAN turns off the set. They sit in silence. OLIVE is frozen in her crushing disappointment. She continues to stare in disbelief at the dark TV screen. SYLVAN, his face registering total sympathy, is completely at one with her.)

ROBERT. *(awkwardly)* Well, you were brilliant. It was a brilliant scene.

TREY. *(trying to be positive)* I don't even see where the other scenes would have been. I mean, it was a very tight, suspenseful show.

WENDY. *(heartbroken)* But they were wonderful scenes.

ROBERT. The one scene left was the emotional high point of the episode.

(SYLVAN subtly gestures to ROBERT to refrain from speaking anymore.

(OLIVE, devastated, gets up from the sofa, slowly crosses to the door and opens it. She's unable to utter a single word. The others, feeling her profound disappointment, rise from their seats. As if attending a funeral, they silently gather up the cheese plate and tapenade.)

(Wishing they could provide OLIVE with some words of comfort, her stricken face makes any platitude seem foolish. They silently file out of the apartment.)

(SYLVAN is the last to leave. He feels for her so deeply and attempts a gesture of affection but OLIVE wearily raises her hand to silence him. Sensitively, he gets the point and leaves.)

(**OLIVE** *returns to the sofa and stares once again at the dark TV screen.*)

End of Scene

Scene Five

(The following morning. **OLIVE**, *still in last night's clothes, is lying on the sofa. She opens her eyes and realizes she's been there all night. The phone rings. She doesn't move to answer it. After four rings, the machine automatically picks up. The doorbell rings. She pauses, considering her next move, gives up and answers the door. It's* **WENDY**.*)*

WENDY. May I please come in?

OLIVE. There's nothing to say.

WENDY. Did you sleep in your clothes? I've been so worried about you. I kept flashing back to your face when you realized that all those scenes were missing.

OLIVE. I'm glad I provided grist for your viewing pleasure. It certainly wasn't on the screen. You should be home packing. You've got a lot of work to do if you're gonna relocate.

WENDY. I'm not going. I'm not taking the job.

OLIVE. You were so over the moon about it.

WENDY. *(upbeat)* Then reality hit. I can't give up my life here. I'm very established in the theatre. And I have my volunteer work. All the ladies I do things for. And you're right. I've got a nice studio apartment in a good neighborhood at a decent rent. I just can't shake everything up. I've made the right decision. What can I do to make you feel better?

OLIVE. I keep asking myself, "Why would they butcher that episode?" "Why?" Those scenes added so much to the story.

WENDY. I agree.

OLIVE. That lovely tender moment with the son. Yeah, it was a bit tangential to the plot, but it said so much about Leah's character.

WENDY. I remember. It was beautiful.

OLIVE. And the scene when she was ready to plead guilty. And the little scene with the husband. Take all that away and what's left but me expressing rage. Anger is the easiest emotion for an actor. Hey, maybe they looked at it in the editing room and thought I stunk.

WENDY. That's impossible.

OLIVE. Perhaps I was over the top. I don't know. There may be a reason I'm never up for dramatic roles.

WENDY. Don't do that to yourself. You were brilliant in those scenes. I looked around and even the crew was moved.

OLIVE. *(emotionally)* What makes me so furious is that I allowed myself to get excited. I should have known better. But the picture in the paper and everyone calling. Then they watch it and think I exaggerated how big my part was. I'm so humiliated. And after the director and the executives on the set told me how extraordinary I was, and they don't even have the goddam decency to phone and warn me that most of my part was cut. You know, I partially blame your late brother.

WENDY. What's that supposed to mean?

OLIVE. Did he show up last night? Was all revealed?

WENDY. No.

OLIVE. He was never here. I was projecting all sorts of nonsense on this so-called "Howard." Hope. Love. So when the picture came out in the paper, stupid me thought it was a cosmic sign.

WENDY. I wanted to believe too.

OLIVE. Lying here on the sofa, I finally remembered where I heard those words. "Upon the full moon, all will be revealed." It was part of an old sausage commercial. I was visiting a medium and that was part of her dialogue. And last night wasn't even a full moon. I got that wrong too. What's been revealed is that nothing's out there. No spirits. No angels. No God. Life is a supermarket going out of business. Grab what you can because nobody's restocking.

WENDY. Has it occurred to you that the director might also be upset about the cuts? You don't know. I bet the writer's devastated at seeing his work eviscerated.

OLIVE. I feel bad for him. He wrote a good script.

WENDY. Why don't you give him a call? What's his name?

OLIVE. Jeffrey something. Jeffrey Beaman. I think I saved the contact sheet.

WENDY. Jeffrey Beaman? When I saw it on the credits, I thought it was familiar.

OLIVE. You know Jeffrey Beaman?

WENDY. He was a friend of Howard's. Was he on the set? Did I meet him?

OLIVE. He was around.

WENDY. Years ago, he wrote and directed a little independent film. It was called – *Ariel's Cup.* Howard and I were supposed to go on the opening day to help boost the gross.

OLIVE. I saw that movie.

WENDY. It won awards.

OLIVE. I didn't realize it was his. You know, I think I was also at the opening day. Isn't that wild? I might have run into you years before I met you. And Howard was there? Maybe I met him.

WENDY. I remember the name of that movie because it was the day Howard died.

OLIVE. What? I might have met Howard the day he died?

WENDY. I don't know because I wasn't there. You see, back then I was helping this actress, Lillian Gurney. I met Howard at the subway and then suddenly I had a feeling I should call and check up on Lillian.

OLIVE. You were helping old actresses even then?

WENDY. Even then. I called her and my sixth sense was right. She'd gone to a voice over audition that morning and fallen. She was very upset. Well, I had to tell Howard that I couldn't go to the movie.

OLIVE. Lillian Gurney. We were often up for the same things. In fact, if I'm correct I may be the reason she fell.

WENDY. How's that possible?

OLIVE. I don't remember what I ate for dinner yesterday but I remember the day I saw *Ariel's Cup.* Earlier that morning I'd been to a voiceover audition. I was in the waiting room along with Lillian Gurney. We got in a huge argument over who had arrived first. Lillian started it. She was so furious she threw her cane at me and tripped over a waste paper basket. Isn't that something? If she hadn't lost her temper with me, she wouldn't have fallen and you would have been at the movie with your brother.

(The doorbell rings.)

It's the super. The bathroom sink never stops trickling. There's always something new.

(She opens the door. It's **ROBERT**, **TREY** *and* **SYLVAN**.*)*

Yeah?

ROBERT. We wanted to see how you were doing?

OLIVE. I'll survive. You left some knives and a cutting board in the kitchen.

SYLVAN. I left the jar of pickled herring. You said you didn't like it.

WENDY. We just discovered an amazing coincidence. The day Howard died, I was supposed to go to a movie with him, but I had to cancel at the last minute because a lady I was helping had an accident. It turns out that not only was Olive also at the movie that day but earlier she was at a voiceover audition with the lady I was helping and inadvertently caused the accident that forced me to miss the movie.

SYLVAN. Olive, that's so remarkably similar to what happened to me backstage at Aunt Bella's farewell performance. Your very presence changes lives.

TREY. I'll tell you something even more interesting. I saw Howard the day he died.

WENDY. You did? Why didn't you tell me?

OLIVE. Why didn't you tell me?

TREY. I didn't want to compete. I mean, you're his sister. And you're his conduit to the mortal world.

ROBERT. I didn't know you saw him again after we met him in Key West.

TREY. I couldn't really tell you, if you, um, know what I mean.

ROBERT. Oh?

TREY. This is rather awkward. Robert and I have a longtime strict policy of "Don't ask, don't tell."

ROBERT. And while I may not have asked, you're still gonna tell.

TREY. I feel like I must. May I continue?

SYLVAN. You've gone this far.

TREY. It was late afternoon. I got out of work early, so I decided to stop in a café around the corner and have a cocktail. Who should walk by but Howard? I called out to him and he came inside. He said he had moved back to the city and was working for Corcoran. He was looking very cute and well, I knew you were going to be working late, so I brought him home with me.

ROBERT. I never thought you'd have sex with someone in our bed. That was one rule I was sure neither of us would ever break.

TREY. *(pleading his case)* He was staying in Astoria. Queens! I was extremely nervous entering the building with him. I was afraid we'd run into that old gossip, Essie, who used to park herself in the lobby all day. Thank God, by some miracle, she wasn't there.

OLIVE. Essie. An awful old crone. We were always at odds. You know, I think I may be responsible for why she wasn't in the lobby that day.

TREY. How is that?

OLIVE. If it's the same day we're talking about, eight years ago, I came home and got into an ugly altercation with Essie. She turned away from me, tripped and popped her meniscus.

WENDY. So basically, you caused two old women to fall down in one day.

SYLVAN. Olive, I sit in awe. You're like a mystical High Priestess who bends time and space.

TREY. Howard and I had a very pleasant siesta. When the news spread that he died, I figured out that I'd been with him that day. I've always felt bad because after we finished fooling around, I became paranoid that you might come home early. I practically threw his clothes at him. We barely said goodbye. Naturally, I wonder if I was the last person to speak to him.

WENDY. You weren't. Because I phoned him around eight pm. And we had a huge fight. He had given a total stranger an antique gold filigreed chain that belonged to our grandmother. I was so fed up with his wildly impulsive gestures that I hung up on him. A few hours later he died and I'm left with horrible guilt feelings. All because of that stupid gold chain. I was probably the last person to speak to him and it was fraught with rage.

(**ROBERT** *catches his reflection in the mirror and decides to speak the truth.*)

ROBERT. Would it help you to know that I may have been the last person to speak to him?

TREY. You?

ROBERT. Yeah.

TREY. You kept in touch with Howard after Key West?

ROBERT. I did.

TREY. I don't believe you.

ROBERT. He found me attractive. And I needed that.

TREY. Because you don't get that from me. So you tricked with Howard and it's all my fault.

ROBERT. I did more than trick with Howard. About a month after we met, I flew back to Key West and spent a long weekend alone with him. I told you I was visiting my cousin in Vermont. But I was with Howard. Actually, I flew down there twice. Both times it was lovely. When he returned to New York, he called. We got together a few times but never at our place.

TREY. So you had a major affair with this guy.

ROBERT. It certainly was major to me. That morning Howard phoned and invited me to a party a screen-writer Jeffrey Beaman was throwing that evening to celebrate the opening of his movie. I really wanted to go, just to see Howard, but what excuse could I give you? I was coming home from the office and heading down Second Avenue. I saw an old woman walking her dog. Just then, another woman turned the corner and the dog suddenly lunged at her causing the owner to trip and fall flat on her face. I helped the old lady up and except for some scratches, she was basically all right. That provided me with my alibi. I phoned you and said I was escorting this woman to the emergency room and that it might take several hours.

TREY. Well, you're just a big, fat liar. Aren't you?

ROBERT. I had to see Howard. It was as if I knew I'd never see him again.

OLIVE. I was the woman the dog lunged at. It was a vicious Doberman. He nearly took a bite out of me.

ROBERT. Well, then, Olive, I wouldn't have been at that party if weren't for you.

SYLVAN. Again, you appear to be the force field at the center of the Universe.

TREY. So after I accepted your lie, you got there and–

ROBERT. It was a wild party. All men.

SYLVAN. Oh my.

ROBERT. There was a roof top terrace with a hot tub.

SYLVAN. Oh my.

ROBERT. Sylvan, please. I found Howard in the hot tub and joined him. Once again, he was so affectionate. Trey, I accept that relationships shift and change. We can be more like friends than lovers. But if you were only more pleasant. You've become so relentlessly sour and negative. You're an armadillo that can't be touched. And the drinking doesn't help. It makes it worse. I refuse to believe this is the real you. The real you is the boy I fell in love with and the man who took such care of me when I was ill. If by patronizing you or keeping you dependent, I'm responsible for the other Trey, then I am truly and deeply sorry.

TREY. So what you're saying is; I've become a nasty, alcoholic queen.

ROBERT. I wouldn't put it that way. Yes.

TREY. Why have you never told me this before?

ROBERT. I didn't want to hurt your feelings. I thought I was protecting you. May I continue?

TREY. I'm an evil, gin-soaked lizard. I can take anything.

ROBERT. There's not much more to say. I had to get back home, so I climbed out of the tub and advised Howard that he shouldn't stay in much longer. He winked and said he'd be careful. And I left. I suppose shortly after that, he had his heart attack.

WENDY. Golly. All of us saw him that day, except for Olive... and of course, Sylvan, who doesn't count.

ROBERT. I left out an interesting detail. Jeffrey had a TV on the terrace. It was set to a music video channel and one of Olive's commercials came on. Howard said that was an amazing coincidence because he had just met you earlier that day at Jeffrey's screening.

TREY. Honestly, how the hell do you remember that?

ROBERT. Because Howard beckoned me to join him in the hot tub by saying...

SYLVAN. "Gimme the sausage."

WENDY. *(to* **OLIVE***)* So you did meet Howard.

OLIVE. Yeah.

WENDY. Why haven't you said anything?

OLIVE. I truly only figured it out a few minutes ago. That afternoon, I left the voiceover studio in Tribeca and since it was a nice day, I walked. I passed by the Cinema Village. There was a crowd of people waiting outside. This fellow asked me for the time. He said he never wore a watch. I don't usually talk to strangers, but we hit it off. We were snapping back and forth with the quips in a very congenial manner. When it was time for his movie to start, he asked if I'd care to join him. Very out of character for me but I said, "Why not?" The movie was cute. However, I think I enjoyed it more because my companion had such an infectious laugh. When the movie was over, neither of us was in a particular hurry. As I said, it was a beautiful day, so we walked across town to the East Village and sat in Tomkins Square Park. All these years, I would have sworn that we never exchanged names. But perhaps I've romanticized and edited the events of that afternoon. Or maybe I'm confused because I've lost a lot of brain cells from my, shall we say, episodes. It's possible he did tell me his name was Howard and that he'd worked in real estate and that he'd lived for a time in Key West. Maybe he did tell me all that. The thing is that none of that information seemed important. What you do? Where you live? What's your name? So what did we talk about for nearly three hours? Well, there was a cluster of tiny sparrows searching for crumbs on the ground in front of us. We gave them names and improvised dialogue between them. Sounds nauseatingly cutesy but that's what we did. He told me his favorite song was "I'll Tell The Man In The Street." I love that song too. So we sang a duet, which segued into "Glad To Be Unhappy" and much of the score of *Kismet.* We spent about a half hour trying to hold a conversation without either of us ever starting a sentence with the word "I." It's very difficult. Try it sometime. Now, you would think that after several hours I would have figured out that he was gay. But I didn't. Despite my long career in show business, I'm still in some ways a rather provincial lady from Yonkers. I just got a kick out of him. And he seemed so taken with me. Most of my life, I've felt I had to be a real *shtarker*. A tough guy. Keep my fists at the ready. But I relaxed them that day. I don't generally like myself but I liked that lady. The afternoon was getting on. What do you do? Exchange phone numbers? Make another date? I think we both knew we shouldn't screw up something so magical by being greedy. I told him that I would never forget that afternoon for the rest of my life. He said, "Well, just to make sure you won't forget me, let me give you something." And he pulled over his head this delicate gold chain. I hadn't noticed it before. It was hidden beneath his sweater. He placed the chain in my hand and said it was terribly old and he wanted me to have it. At that moment, for the first and only time, I knew what it was like to love and be loved. We kissed each other goodbye and I walked away.

(She tenderly reveals the gold chain that she's been wearing around her neck and under her blouse. There is a moment of silence)

SYLVAN. We're all a part of God's perfect plan.

TREY. Amen.

ROBERT. I think it was Melville who wrote "We cannot live only for ourselves. A thousand fibers connect us with our fellow men."

WENDY. And now at long last, my Grandmother Minnie's precious gold chain can be restored to me.

(She reaches out her hand.)

OLIVE. Are you nuts? I'm not giving it to you.

WENDY. You've got to. It belonged to my grandmother Minnie.

OLIVE. – who gave it to your brother, who in turn gave it to me.

WENDY. He had no right to do so.

OLIVE. He had every right. If he had gotten married he would have passed it on to his child.

WENDY. But he wasn't married to you or got you knocked up. You met him once, went to the movies and sat in the park. If you had a scintilla of compassion, you would hand over that necklace pronto.

OLIVE. If you had an ounce of sensitivity, you would understand that this chain has enormous emotional profundity to me. Look. How's this? I'll stipulate in my will that upon my death, it should go to you.

SYLVAN. Ladies, that's a reasonable compromise.

WENDY. I can't wait that long. I think you're being incredibly selfish. Your acceptance of that necklace destroyed my last moments with my brother and now you deny me the closure I so desperately seek.

OLIVE. Oh my, how you're carrying on. Get over it.

WENDY. Give me that necklace or I'll take you to court.

OLIVE. You'd lose.

TREY. Give her the goddam necklace.

OLIVE. This is none of your affair.

ROBERT. It is our affair. Four of us shared that last day with Howard.

OLIVE. *(sincerely)* But I'm the only one whose time with him meant anything.

WENDY. You miserable bitch. Everything has to be about you. You, you, you. I'm sick of you.

OLIVE. Now the venom is released.

WENDY. For months, you've bossed and bullied me. I was warned that you were a horror. But I felt pity for you. The same as I felt for all the other mean spirited old ladies I've slaved for. Sylvia Samuels, Lillian Gurney, Doris Blau, Grace Chen. I get this insane notion that I can make a difference. Guys, you see that notebook on the desk? I wrote in it the phone numbers of all sorts of places that could improve Olive's depressing solitary existence. Opportunities to do volunteer work, to teach, to build herself up physically. She's never even opened that notebook. All for naught. Well, I've had it. I'm going.

TREY. Where? I'll go with you.

WENDY. *(with feverish intensity)* I'm going to LA. I'm taking that job. Oh, yes. And I'm going to be young. I'm going to learn to para-sail off the Pacific coast. I'm going to roller blade on Santa Monica pier. I'm going to ride the waves at Zuma Beach. And for at least the next fifteen years, I never want to hear the phrase, "I'm getting a chill," or, "I feel the humidity in my bones." I never want to hear, "Make me some tea." "Is the meat lean?" "Don't I get a discount?" The chains of bondage are broken. The waters have parted. Free at last! Free at last! Oh, dear Lord, I'm free at last!

OLIVE. She's not going anywhere.

*(**WENDY** looks once more at **OLIVE** very clearly and exits.)*

ROBERT. Olive, you've lost a good friend. Come on, Trey. Let's go home.

TREY. You really want me with you? I broke a cardinal rule.

ROBERT. Can you forgive me for telling so many lies? I thought I was protecting you.

TREY. You don't have to protect me. I won't break.

ROBERT. Let's try to be more forthright.

TREY. I had sex with your cousin Monty.

ROBERT. Monty's gay?

TREY. A troubled bisexual. It was grisly.

ROBERT. I had sex with Mark Novello.

TREY. Mark Novello? Who was Mark Novello?

ROBERT. Your gastroenterologist.

TREY. You had sex with Dr. Novello?

ROBERT. Are you very upset?

TREY. He's gorgeous. Was he any good? Hairy chest? Big dick? Circumcised? *(to **OLIVE**)* We've got to go.

ROBERT. There are more truths to be told. Olive, I don't like you. I tried but I'll never like you.

TREY. Now, it's my turn. Olive, you're toxic. And that kind of poisonous behavior is contagious. I'm susceptible to it, so I can't come anywhere near you. And if you start banging on the wall again, we'll simply call the police. Goodbye.

ROBERT. Goodbye.

(**TREY** *links his arm in* **ROBERT**'s *and they exit.*)

SYLVAN. They're all speaking in the heat of anger.

OLIVE. I could care less. I'm me. Olive Blechman. I can't change my DNA. So, fella, you can also take your leave.

SYLVAN. Why me? What did I do?

OLIVE. There's something wrong with you. You go after these difficult women, because what? You're missing something in your own personality? Your mother was right. How many times do you have to get kicked in the ass?

SYLVAN. *(simply)* I always think I can help.

OLIVE. You're like a vampire. You want my anger and spirit. Well, you can't have 'em.

SYLVAN. You need to be loved. And not by a dead person, but a live human being. I'm not even suggesting that it might be me. But look to the living. They're out there.

OLIVE. That's a ridiculous over simplification. I'm not a character in a Yiddish folk tale.

SYLVAN. Olive –

OLIVE. This conversation is terminated.

SYLVAN. You gotta have the last word. Don't you?

OLIVE. I don't.

SYLVAN. You do.

OLIVE. I don't.

SYLVAN. You do.

SYLVAN. Come here.

(*He pulls her towards the decorative mirror.*)

OLIVE. What are you doing?

SYLVAN. There we are.

OLIVE. I thought there was nothing in that mirror for you.

SYLVAN. I like the way we look together.

OLIVE. Sylvan, it's too late. It's always been too late.

SYLVAN. Perhaps I'm Howard's instrument on earth. Ever think of that?

OLIVE. I'm not in the market to be loved.

SYLVAN. No one should be allowed to say that.

OLIVE. I'm unlovable. I can give you references. Now, I'm asking you to leave.

SYLVAN. I never thought I'd say this, but I, for one, am looking forward to a restful time in Argentina.

(He exits. **OLIVE** *is alone. She looks in the mirror and searches for Howard.)*

OLIVE. No way am I giving her this chain. She'll just have to get over it in sunny right wing California. Who needs her? And I certainly don't need those two next door. Or Carol Kandel's father. I'm a very self reliant woman. Always have been.

(She notices the notebook on the table. She opens it.)

OLIVE. What am I supposed to do with all this? *(She dials the first number and waits.)*

PHONE. *(RING...RING...PICKUP.)*

OLIVE. Hello, Milton Keisler Acting Studios? This is —

PHONE. Thank you for calling Milton Keisler Acting Studios. For Administration, Press one. For directions and hours, press two.

OLIVE. —A machine… Administration. Press one.

PHONE. *(RING...RING...PICKUP.)*

OLIVE. Hello, this is Olive Fi –

PHONE. No one is currently available to take your call. To leave a message, press one. Otherwise, call back during office hours, Monday-Friday, 10-5pm.

OLIVE. Who the hell do they think they are? Okay. I'll just leave a message.

PHONE. *(BEEP)*

OLIVE. This is Olive Fisher. I'm interested in teaching a class in acting for commercials. I have over thirty years of experience and have landed numerous national spots. Oh for Christ sake. I'm the "Gimme the sausage" lady. You can reach me at 212 691 8389. *(She hangs up.)* Okay. Let's see what else do we have here? That's stupid. What the hell was she thinking? *(She dials another number.)*

PHONE. *(RING...PICKUP)* Integral Yoga *(Pause)* –

OLIVE. Hello? I'd like to sign up for a yoga class. What times are the –

PHONE. – For class information, press one.

OLIVE. One…

PHONE. *(RING....PICKUP)* For teacher directory, press one. To book a class, press two.

OLIVE. Two…

PHONE. *(PICKUP)*

OLIVE. Hello?

PHONE. To book a class, please leave your message after the beep.

OLIVE. Here we go again.

PHONE. *(BEEP)*

OLIVE. My name is Olive Fisher. I'm interested in taking a Yoga class. Please call me at 212 691 8389.

(She hangs up and looks at the list again. She dials.)

(The doorbell rings.)

OLIVE. Now the super comes. *(Shouts)* Door's open!

(Focused on her phone call, she doesn't immediately see **SYLVAN** *enter the apartment.)*

PHONE. *(RING. PICKUP)* Hello. Thank you for calling.

OLIVE. Hello? Hello? Is this the Jewish Federation for the Blind?

PHONE. You've reached the volunteer program. Please leave a message after the beep.

OLIVE. Another recording.

(**OLIVE** *looks up and sees* **SYLVAN**. *He tries to suppress his delight at seeing her reaching out to the world. Feeling remarkably at home, he stretches out on the sofa.* **OLIVE**, *inwardly amused at his pleasure, continues on the phone and perhaps is even performing a bit for her audience of one.*)

PHONE. *(BEEP)*

OLIVE. My name is Olive Fisher. I'm a professional actress and I'd like to read or record for the blind.

PHONE. Please say "yes" for further options.

OLIVE. Yes…I can't believe this. When I get someone on the line, they're gonna wish they were deaf…

PHONE. If you are calling about home visits, say "yes".

OLIVE. …No…This is ludicrous. I have a lot to offer. I'll take my talents elsewhere.

(*She sits in the middle of the sofa in front of* **SYLVAN**'s *reclining figure.*)

PHONE. To re-record your message, say "yes".

OLIVE. No…This is cruel and inhumane.

PHONE. Would you like to hear a recorded schedule of weekly programming?

OLIVE. No! Please, for the love of God, let me talk to a LIVE HUMAN BEING!

(**SYLVAN** *begins kissing her free arm.*)

PHONE. I'm sorry, I didn't understand that. Would you like to speak to an operator?

OLIVE. Yes!

PHONE. I'm sorry, I didn't understand that. Would you like to speak to an operator?

(**SYLVAN** *continues his journey kissing her arm.* **OLIVE** *succumbs to his advances.*)

OLIVE. *(giggling)* Yes!

PHONE. I'm sorry, I didn't understand that. Would you like to speak to an operator?

*(**SYLVAN** pulls **OLIVE** down on top of him on the sofa.)*

OLIVE. YES! YES! YES!

*(Lights fade out on **OLIVE**, laughing in sensual pleasure and at the absurdity of the situation and making a concerted attempt to change her life. Perhaps a faint warm glow is seen in the mirror.)*

End of Play

Also by
Charles Busch...

Die Mommie Die!

The Divine Sister

The Green Heart

The Lady in Question

Our Leading Lady

Psycho Beach Party

Queen Amarantha

Red Scare on Sunset

Shanghai Moon

Sleeping Beauty or Coma

Swingtime Canteen

Tale of the Allergist's Wife

The Third Story

Times Square Angel

Vampire Lesbians of Sodom

You Should Be So Lucky

OTHER TITLES AVAILABLE FROM SAMUEL FRENCH

RED SCARE ON SUNSET

Charles Busch

Comedy / 5m, 3f / Unit Set

This Off-Broadway hit is set in 1950's Hollywood during the blacklist days. This is a hilarious comedy that touches on serious subjects by the author of *Vampire Lesbians of Sodom.*

Mary Dale is a musical comedy star who discovers to her horror that her husband, her best friend, her director and houseboy are all mixed up in a communist plot to take over the movie industry. Among their goals is the dissolution of the star system! Mary's conversion from Rodeo Drive robot to McCarthy marauder who ultimately names names, including her husband's, makes for outrageous, thought provoking comedy. The climax is a wild dream sequence where Mary imagines she's Lady Godiva, the role in the musical she's currently filming. Both right and left are skewered in this comic melodrama.

"You have to champion the ingenuity of Busch's writing which twirls twist upon twist and spins into comedy heaven."
– *Newsday*

OTHER TITLES AVAILABLE FROM SAMUEL FRENCH

THE TALE OF THE ALLERGIST'S WIFE

Charles Busch

Comedy / 2m, 3f / Interior

Winner of the Outer Critics Circle John Gassner Award.

An award winning hit at the Manhattan Theatre Club and on Broadway, *The Tale of the Allergist's Wife* is a radical departure for the well known author of extravagant spoofs like *Vampire Lesbians of Sodom* and *Psycho Beach Party*. Marjorie Taub, the wife of a philanthropic allergist, is engulfed in a life crisis of Medea-like proportions. Her children are grown, her beloved therapist died recently and her mother, obsessed with bowel movements, grates on her nerves. She tries to lose herself in a world of art galleries, foreign films and avant garde theatre, but finds she is barely able to rouse herself from her sofa. Her spirits suddenly soar when a fascinating and incredibly worldly friend from her childhood appears on her doorstep. Lee the savior that infuses Marjorie with life becomes Lee the unwelcome and sinister guest in short order.

"A window rattling comedy of mid life malaise...Mr. Busch has swum straight into the mainstream...*The Allergist's Wife* earns its wall to wall laughs."
– *The New York Times*

"Charles Busch comes of age as a comic playwright of the first rank."
– *The New York Daily News*

"An intelligently funny and satirically relevant uptown comedy."
– *New York Magazine*

OTHER TITLES AVAILABLE FROM SAMUEL FRENCH

THE DIVINE SISTER

Charles Busch

Comedy / 1m, 5f / Multiple Sets

Nominee! Off Broadway Alliance Award for Best New Play

The Divine Sister is an outrageous comic homage to nearly every Hollywood film involving nuns. Evoking such films as *The Song of Bernadette, The Bells of St. Mary's, The Singing Nun* and *Agnes of God, The Divine Sister* tells the story of St. Veronica's indomitable Mother Superior who is determined to build a new school for her Pittsburgh convent. Along the way, she has to deal with a young postulant who is experiencing "visions," sexual hysteria among her nuns, a sensitive schoolboy in need of mentoring, a mysterious nun visiting from the Mother House in Berlin, and a former suitor intent on luring her away from her vows.

This madcap trip through Hollywood religiosity evokes the wildly comic but affectionately observed theatrical style of the creator of *Die, Mommie, Die!* and *Psycho Beach Party.*

"Cue the "Hallelujah" chorus! Charles Busch has put on a nun's habit and is talking to God, from whom he has evidently received blessed counsel. *The Divine Sister,* his new comedy at the SoHo Playhouse, finds Mr. Busch at peak form. This gleefully twisted tale of the secret lives of nuns — in which the playwright doubles as leading lady — is Mr. Busch's freshest, funniest work in years, perhaps decades."
– *The New York Times*

OTHER TITLES AVAILABLE FROM SAMUEL FRENCH

GREEN HEART

Book by Charles Busch
Music and Lyrics by Rusty Magee
Based on the story by Jack Ritchie

Musical Comedy / 2m, 3f / Multiple Sets

This camp comedy thriller of greed and romance is about an Ivy League playboy who has squandered his fortune. Assisted by his girlfriend, he schemes to restore his wealth by wedding a botany crazed spinster heiress. He discovers that her conniving lawyer and sinister housekeeper are already robbing her blind and know that he plans to bump her off to become a merry widower. Soon, murder is clumsily afoot, alliances are formed and reformed, and plans that do not come to fruition bare unexpected fruit.

"Plump with funny lines."
– *The New York Times*

"Funny! Inventive! Outrageously outrageous!"
– *New York Post*

"Plenty of laughs."
– *New York Daily News*

"Playful, funny and original!"
– *Gannett Newspapers*

"Demented and delightful...The jauntiest musical since Little Shop."
– *Newsday*

OTHER TITLES AVAILABLE FROM SAMUEL FRENCH

THE THIRD STORY

Charles Busch

Comedy / 4m, 2f / Unit Set

A faded screenwriter in the 1940's woos her troubled ex-writer son into collaborating on a screen play. The gangster/sci fi B-movie in their imagination unfolds before us, involving a chic crime czarina, a beautiful but icy lady scientist and her failed and understandably bitter human cloning experiment. A third story is the Russian fairy tale the screenwriter told her son as a child about a painfully shy princess who forges a diabolical pact with a terrifying but surprisingly vulnerable old witch. The fairy tale inspires the movie which inspires the mother and son screenwriters to mend their fractured relationship.

"Plays-within-plays require such intricate tailoring. So it's a pleasure to report that with *The Third Story*, the ever-captivating Charles Busch proves equally deft as both performer and seamstress."
– *TheaterMania.com*

"The main joy of *The Third Story* is that its foolery embodies something substantive...No wonder *The Third Story* feels like such an energizing event."
– *Village Voice*